OTHER BOOKS BY CHRIS STEWART

A Christmas Bell for Anya

The Fourth War

The God of War

The Kill Box

The Miracle of Freedom: 7 Tipping Points That Saved the World

Seven Miracles That Saved America

Shattered Bone

The Third Consequence

Wrath and Righteousness, episodes 1–9

WINTER SKY

A NOVEL

CHRIS STEWART

Coat of arms: © SimeonVD/shutterstock.com

Visit us at ShadowMountain.com

Library of Congress Cataloging-in-Publication Data

Names: Stewart, Chris, 1960– author.
Title: Winter sky / Chris Stewart.
Description: Salt Lake City, Utah : Shadow Mountain, [2016]
Identifiers: LCCN 2016021339 | ISBN 9781629722290 (hardbound : alk. paper)
Subjects: LCSH: World War, 1939–1945—Underground movements—Poland—Fiction. | Amnesiacs—Fiction. | War and families—Poland—Fiction.
Classification: LCC PS3569.T4593 W56 2016 | DDC 813/.54—dc23
LC record available at https://lccn.loc.gov/2016021339

Printed in the United States of America
Publishers Printing, Salt Lake City, UT

10 9 8 7 6 5 4 3 2 1

To those who know that life is full of surprises,
and that sometimes those surprises are good.

When I consider thy heavens, the work of thy fingers,
the moon and the stars, which thou hast ordained;
What is man, that thou art mindful of him?
and the son of man, that thou visitest him?

–PSALM 8:3–4

The Spirit itself beareth witness with our spirit,
that we are the children of God.

–ROMANS 8:16

INTRODUCTION

By December 1944, World War II was coming to a violent and chaotic end. Seventy million people had already died in the greatest upheaval of nations that the world had ever seen. No continent was untouched, no nation unaffected. But the dying was not yet over, for the Nazis did not intend to fade quietly into the night. Hitler was determined to fight to the very last man, seemingly convinced that, in the end, the sheer power of his will would prevail, that miracles of darkness were coming, that the gods were on his side. So his defeated army warred on like a deflating lung inside a dying body, slowly collapsing under the weight of the mighty Allied forces that were crushing it from all sides.

From Stalingrad to London, from Jerusalem to Tokyo, and every spot in between, nations collided in the final stages of war. In the wake, armies were left abandoned, rebels rose, and cities were destroyed, leaving chaos everywhere.

As the Third Reich collapsed, Stalin moved to fill the void. And he was just getting started, having twenty million of his fellow men yet to kill. He controlled more than two million battle-hardened men, twenty-five hundred tanks, and more artillery than anyone could even count. It was, perhaps, the largest army ever assembled. And the Russians were not a docile lot. Quite the opposite. They swept in from the east with many reasons to be furious: the death of millions of their countrymen, the rape of their motherland, the pain they had endured, and the hunger and deprivation they had suffered. Indignant with rage, they were determined to destroy more than just the fleeing German army. Ukraine. Hungary. Latvia. The Czechs. Many were in Stalin's determined path. And the Russians claimed no friends; their world was only potential enemies—nations to be occupied and people to be destroyed.

Out of all the nations that lay in Russia's path, none but the Nazis were more hated than the Poles.

Ironically, none had suffered as much as the Polish people had. Six million men, women, and children had been lost in the war, almost 20 percent of the country's entire population. And the Poles knew that, as bad as the Nazi occupation had been, the approaching Russians were no better.

For years, a small cadre of Polish rebels had proven themselves effective in harassing the mighty Nazi army from the protection of the hills and thick forests of the rural regions. As the Nazis fell back, this small group of determined men turned their expertise in guerrilla tactics toward the coming Russian army, hoping against all odds to claim a free Poland for themselves.

They knew that it was a nearly hopeless endeavor, but still they fought on.

The Russians did not take kindly to this.

As the winter of 1944 settled in, it became obvious that the rebels were doomed to fail. The brutal Russian IV Corps was too effective and battle tested. It took only a few months for their forces to bring the rebels to their knees. Soon the Polish fighters were running out of ammunition, food, and supplies. By the time the first snow settled on the mountains, they were nearly out of men.

PROLOGUE

SOUTHERN POLAND

DECEMBER 16, 1944

The heavy shelling suddenly stopped, the horrific bursts of black powder and steel no longer raining metal and death upon the ground. Terrible moments of silence followed, black and still as the crystal winter sky.

The stillness continued for several gut-wrenching moments.

The German medic understood what this meant. He stared in terror at the sky. The enemy was getting ready to send its army in. It was standard practice: soften the target with artillery—or, much more likely with the Russians, beat it into merciless devastation—then stop the shelling and send in the troops to finish the job.

The corpsman stood without moving, his heartbeat surging in his ears, his eyes unfocused, his weary arms hanging loosely at his sides. He was utterly exhausted. It seemed too much effort even to breathe. He closed his eyes as he stood, but felt himself wobble into sleep and forced himself to open them again.

He listened. The winter night was cold and clear. He cocked his head, ignoring the moaning all around him, filtering the sound of the human suffering as he strained to hear the enemy's approach. He heard the *whoosh* of the gas lanterns that were hanging on the walls. He heard the soft breeze that brushed across the sides of the canvas tent. In the distance, he heard the sound of heavy engines, the last of his German comrades as they began their retreat. The rumble of their transport and tank engines quickly faded in the cold wind.

He glanced at his surroundings. The military field hospital was utter chaos: gear, tattered cloth, dirty bandages, and bodies, a few dead, a few who were barely living. There were no longer any doctors, only he, a single corpsman, and a couple of aides remained, all of them surrounded by far more wounded than they could ever hope to help.

The muddy earth beneath the creamy canvas of the tent was slippery-red from the blood of the dead and dying men who had been placed there over the past twenty hours. Along one wall of the tent, four bodies had been laid side by side, their faces covered with their own jackets. Who was going to bury them? The corpsman didn't know. Russian soldiers were the only option, but they weren't any good at such things, not even for their own men, and certainly not for the hated enemy. These four would likely be pushed into a shallow trench and covered with a thin layer of dirt. To his left was a makeshift operating table, bare pine and crossed beams with rusty nails. A dead man lay upon the table, his left leg entirely blown off.

One of the aides, an enlisted boy who had been trained to shoot a rifle, dig a trench, and very little else, lay in a heap of exhaustion on the floor. Two other aides started to lift the dead man off the table.

"Ein . . . zwie," one of them counted as they prepared to lift.

The other one looked up with wild eyes. *"Sie kommen. Wir haben zu gehen!"* (They're coming. We have to go!)

"Nein! Wir können sie nicht verlassen!" (No! We can't leave them.)

They froze, holding the limp body in midair.

Silence. The terrifying silence.

"If we leave them, they will die!"

"If we stay here, *we* die as well!"

The lead corpsman motioned for them to get back to work. "One more man," he commanded.

Not more than twenty years of age, the corpsman was the oldest soldier in the room. His face was covered in dirt and blood and a wisp of unshaved beard. He nodded to his aides. "Him. Up on the table." They dropped the dead man beside the others, then plopped another wounded soldier up on the blood-soaked table. The injured man was unconscious from all of the morphine he'd been given before being dragged into the field hospital. A *hospital!* the corpsman snorted, as if a single tent with no doctor, equipment, or medicine could be called such a thing.

Behind him, a young German soldier lay unconscious in the mud. The corpsman glanced at him. Blond hair. Mud on his face. Blood oozing from both ears. He walked to him and leaned over, lifted an eyelid to examine the dilated pupil, then straightened up and listened once again.

Far off in the distance, a heavy burst of machine-gun fire shattered the eerie silence.

He cocked his head, trying to pinpoint the location of the shooting while knowing that it had to have come from the top of the ridge, two or three hundred meters to the east. As if on cue, the canvas above his head suddenly split as the first rounds of machine-gun fire tore through the fabric. He hesitated. Another burst of 20-caliber cut through the tattered canvas. A gas lantern exploded, the fuel spilling across the ground. A cold wind blew, smoky and rich with the smell of gunpowder and wet earth.

Two German soldiers suddenly appeared at the flap in the tent. Dark uniforms. Short machine guns. Arrogant. Determined. *Special Security* patches on their uniforms.

"What are you doing?" the medic demanded.

They ignored him, taking in the death and blood with fearless eyes.

The first German spotted the blond soldier and moved toward him. The second followed. The first one knelt and put his cheek next to the wounded man's face, feeling for his breath.

"He's alive," he said.

"Who are you?" the medic cried. "Get out of here!"

A sudden burst of artillery fire exploded in the dark. Dirt and metal blew against the canvas tent. The corpsmen fell to the mud, one of them screaming in fear. The German soldiers didn't seem to notice.

The second German stepped over the wounded soldier and knelt beside him too. He felt his chest, prodded his stomach, then rolled him to his side and felt along his spine.

He nodded to his comrade. "Together," he said as he placed both hands along the wounded man's back. "Try to keep his neck straight."

His partner reached down, and they lifted him together.

"Leave him!" the medic screamed in fury. "He will die if you . . ."

Gunfire tore through the fabric once again. The medic fell silent. The soldiers carried the wounded man toward the tent flap that was snapping in the wind. The first soldier glanced back. "You don't have much time," he said. "Do what you can for the others, then get out of here."

With the wounded man in their arms, the Germans pushed the canvas flap aside and disappeared.

ONE

She was young and pretty and suffering from hunger and cold. He was even younger, frail and afraid. With the same dark hair and dark eyes, they were obviously siblings; it was equally obvious that they were alone. They stood beside the horse-drawn wagon and looked up anxiously. The old woman looked down at them, her sizable weight compressing the metal springs as she leaned over the edge of the wooden seat. "You be alone?" she questioned wearily, knowing the answer before she even asked.

The little girl nodded.

"How old?" the woman demanded.

"I'm twelve!" the girl said defiantly.

Her younger brother kept his eyes down but slowly shook his head. The old woman snorted. She didn't need the boy to know that his older sister had just lied. The girl was eight, maybe nine at the oldest. But the old woman didn't care. She had seen so many orphaned children. Hundreds. A thousand. Enough that her heart couldn't break for their suffering any longer. "Where are you going?" she asked them harshly. The conversation was taking too much time. She glanced nervously around, her eyes darting down the road while her old mare bent back her ears and turned her head anxiously toward a nearby grove of leafless trees.

"Gorndask," the girl answered.

"Why there? Do you have family?"

The little boy shook his head again. "We're going to Brzeg, Cela," he corrected.

"Aron!" the girl exclaimed in frustration.

The woman snorted again. The boy seemed to have a fixation on being honest, a fine trait at times, but not in the dying days of war.

The old woman nodded to the south and frowned. "Brzeg is too far. Too dangerous." She pointed a meaty finger down the muddy road. "Gorndask. That's as far as you're going to make it. Stay there. Don't even try to get to Brzeg. You will die out on the roads if you try to go that far."

She turned forward in the wagon seat and picked up the reins. The horse was instantly alert, ready for her command, but before she snapped the leather straps she reached under the seat. Pulling out a burlap sack, she took out a loaf of braided bread and handed it to the children. They took the bread hungrily, their eyes wide with surprise. It was like a miracle from heaven. "*Dziekuje!*" the little girl cried with relief as they tore into the loaf.

The woman nodded at them, then snapped the reins, and the old horse lifted her plodding feet. As the wagon rolled away, the woman glanced back at the orphaned children. She wanted to tell them that someone in Gorndask would help them. She wanted to tell them that they would be safe there.

But she didn't tell them anything, for she knew none of that was true.

TWO

OUTSIDE OF GORNDASK, POLAND
DECEMBER 20, 1944

The train swayed abruptly as it lurched along the poorly repaired tracks. Rail lines were the lifeblood of the war effort, and for six years the line, like every other in the war zone, had fallen under relentless bombing attack. Indeed, the track had been bombed and rebuilt so many times it was a miracle that it could carry any rail traffic at all. So the train engineer kept it slow, knowing that every bridge was an adventure, every crossing a potential derailing point. At one junction he looked briefly for oncoming traffic, though he suspected his was the only train running within two hundred miles. Who else would have the courage, or desperation, or defiance, or whatever combination of such things it might take to put another train upon the track?

The railroad track was a thread of black weaving through a white and green landscape of rolling hills, thick forests, farming cottages, and small towns. Black smoke billowed from the engine and floated back to coat the train in gray soot. The countryside was white with fresh snow. The storm had started out as rain a couple of days before and then turned to heavy snow, thick and wet. The train was surrounded by tall pines, their boughs drooping under the snow's weight, seeming to reach for the ground. The sky was cloudy still, gray with soft wisps of fog drifting over the hills. Winter had come, and it might be weeks before the sun would break through the overcast to sparkle on the snow.

The train consisted of five troop transport cars. All the seats had long before been ripped out, leaving the desperate passengers to stand chest-to-chest or back-to-back as they swayed together with each lurch of the train. A few of the weakest among them huddled on the floor, too exhausted, sick, or wounded to stand.

The cars were packed with terrified civilians, mostly women and their scarce belongings: piles of clothing held together with rope, a few bags, an occasional suitcase. One of the women held a small sewing machine, another a wooden cage stuffed with three chickens. In the corner of the compartment, a young mother stood alone. Her long hair framed a beautiful oval face that was so vacant it looked lifeless. In her arms, she held a tiny bundle tightly wrapped from head to toe in a light blue baby blanket. Her child. No longer living. Taking him home. It was a pitiful sight, and the other passengers gave her as much space as they could muster, but no one spoke to her. The death of a child was as common as the falling of the snow, and no one had the ability to offer any comfort anymore.

To the west, the Germans had turned to take a final stand at the border of the Fatherland. To the east, less than twenty miles away, the mighty Russian army was approaching. The passengers were caught between the pincers, and most of them felt the chaos of war would never end. All of them were hungry. All of them were cold. And their only hope of survival was to flee the coming Russian horde.

In the back corner of the last troop compartment, a group of men stood together, tense, their eyes darting about. They were ragged and hungry like the others, with beards and rough hands. No one knew them, but everyone knew who they were. There was only one possible explanation for a group of men such as this traveling together: Devil's Rebels. The insurrection. Those brave young men and others like them had been raining hell upon the Germans for the last six years. There were a dozen of them in all, ragged individuals in mismatched and poorly fitting clothes. And though the travelers considered every one of them a hero, no one acknowledged them in any way. It was far too dangerous to be seen consorting with the hated enemy of the Nazis.

Two of the rebels stood together. Four days before, under heavy fire and wearing stolen German uniforms, they had slipped into a German field hospital to rescue one of their own. They stood on both sides of the young man now, occasionally reaching up to brace him as the train swayed along the rickety track.

The wounded man stared blankly into space, one eye unfocused, a smear of blood still oozing from his left ear. His blond hair was long and hung in front of his brown eyes. His face was square, with a prominent nose and dark skin. He was tall and almost thin from too many exhausting days and not enough to eat. And though his eyes were bleary, they contained an innocence that was rare in this part of the world. In the middle of a war zone, in a place where everyone was guilty of something in the desperate struggle to survive, very few were innocent any longer. Yet he seemed to have escaped some of the evil, and that made him look out of place.

He reached up and touched the blood on his cheeks. *Why are my ears bleeding?* his brain screamed in pain.

He stared in confusion at the blood on the tip of his finger. His legs felt like water, and waves of nausea heaved up inside him. He hadn't eaten anything in the last two days, and that was good, for he surely would have lost it all from the sickness and disorientation that rolled from his stomach to his head. He lifted his hands, which were shaking badly, then jammed them into the pockets of a discarded military jacket that wasn't his.

Why does my head spin? Why does my body hurt? his brain screamed again.

He didn't know it, but a Russian shell had landed less than ten feet from where he had been bending over one of his wounded friends. His head hurt because it had nearly been torn off his shoulders, throwing his brain against the back of his skull like a pile of jelly against the side of a bowl. His feet hurt because the bones had nearly been broken from the shock wave that had spread across the ground from the exploding artillery shell. His chest hurt from the enormous pressure that had overinflated his lungs. His hands trembled from the nerve damage along his spine.

If he could have remembered, he would have realized that he was lucky to be alive. If he could have remembered, he would know that, even in the midst of the battle, he hadn't been afraid. If he could have remembered, he would have admitted that wasn't because he was particularly brave but because of the fact that, after six years of bitter fighting, he had reached the point where he approached death much like a very old man: he knew it was coming, he just didn't know when. Maybe today, maybe tomorrow, but it was not far away.

But he didn't have any of those feelings because he couldn't remember anything.

He stood with the other men, trembling hands stuffed inside his pockets. Fragmented images continued to flash through his mind. *Faces of children. An unknown stranger. A wounded soldier in his arms.*

Who was it? He didn't know!

A church. A military truck. Dozens of German tanks lined up along a road that ran through a thick forest.

He couldn't remember where it was!

An open field scattered with wildflowers and deep ruts of exploded dirt. The sound of screaming aircraft engines. A little girl crying. A soft hand inside his own.

None of it meant anything!

He nearly panicked from the confusion, having to force himself to breathe.

The train lurched and he stumbled, wondering how much longer he could stand. He glanced down at his clothes, a winter jacket, a brown scarf, and mismatched gloves. His breath formed light clouds of mist that were quickly blown away in the drafty railcar. No one spoke to him as they rocked along.

Inside his jacket pocket, he fingered a photograph, the thick paper rough against his fingers. He touched it tenderly. It was the most important thing he owned. No, that wasn't right. It was the *only* thing he owned. He carefully pulled it out, hiding it inside cupped hands. Crinkled. Dirty. Smeared with a thin line of dried blood. Worst of all, it was torn in two, the right side nothing but a jagged edge. He studied it a moment, then stuffed it protectively back inside his pocket.

The train slowed, the engine belching black smoke. All the windows in the troop cars had been replaced with wooden slats and then covered with metal bars. Small openings between the rough slats allowed the passengers to look out. The rebels stared through the slats as a tattered village came into view when the train emerged from the cover of the woods. "Looks like Gorndask," one of them said.

"Or what is left of it," another answered softly.

A couple of the civilians also turned to look between the slats, a silence seeming to fall upon them.

"It is a hard place," one of them muttered. "These people have borne more than their share of the war."

One of the soldiers nodded to the one who was bleeding from his ear. "Someone said this was his village," he said.

The wounded man leaned over and stared between the slats, taking in the small town as the train passed through scattered openings in the trees. *My village!* he thought through the pounding in his head. *How could this be my village? I don't recognize anything!*

The commander of the rebel unit, someone they would have called lieutenant if he had been wearing a uniform, studied the shell-shocked rebel. "I don't know what to think of him anymore," he said to no one in particular.

One of the other soldiers answered. "Shell-shocked, sir. Concussion. Maybe worse."

The lieutenant scowled. "I can't be responsible for a witless soldier."

His sergeant nodded. Neither could he. Still, he hunched a weary shoulder. He knew there was more to the soldier than an injury to his head. He had seen it before—far too often, in fact. The violence and destruction had finally taken its toll, and if the wounded kid wasn't completely broken, then he was right on the edge. But that was what happened when they sent such young men into war. So he spoke up to defend him. "He's a good soldier. He volunteered for the resistance. That says a lot, especially for someone so young."

"Young!" the lieutenant snorted. "I've seen children fight this war."

"He isn't much more than that even now, and he's been fighting for many years." The soldier paused. "And he risked his life to save me."

"Then you saved him at the field hospital. I think you're even now."

"Maybe that's enough. Maybe the rest of it doesn't really matter."

They rode along in silence as the train slowed, the boxcars clattering with each passing section of track. The air inside the boxcar was humid with human sweat and breath. The lieutenant glanced in the direction of the approaching Russian army. A million men were coming. He glanced to the west, knowing the Germans were waiting there. He was so tired of the fighting. It had been so long. Six years of fighting the hated Nazis. Six months of fighting the hated Russians. War was all he knew. Friend after friend and death after death. "We've got nothing left to fight for," he finally whispered to himself.

"The only thing we're fighting for now is to live," his sergeant answered.

"What are we going to tell our children?"

"That we fought beside our brothers."

"And we lost them all for nothing."

The train continued to slow, clattering at a crawl along the tracks.

The lieutenant nodded to the wounded man. "Even if we had somebody left to fight, he's no good to any of us now."

The sergeant didn't reply.

The train jerked a final time and came to a halt. They had to stop for water for the steam engine, but no one would be let off the train. And they wouldn't stop for long. Their destination was many miles to the south. Almost all the passengers were trying to make their way back to Warsaw, where they had had families before the war. Most of them wouldn't make it. The train was only going halfway, and the roads were controlled by either the Nazis or the Russians, depending on the area and the day. The train would draw an enormous amount of attention, which in the middle of a war was never good. But for most of them, it was their only choice. It was this or walk all the way to Warsaw through the winter.

The engine hissed as the engineer released pressure on the brakes. The lieutenant had to make a quick decision. "You think this is his home?" he pressed again.

"Who knows? Maybe. That's what someone said."

The commander turned away in thought. A deep sadness seemed to fall upon him, darkening his face. He sighed in resignation. "Leave him here. Let him go and find his home." He paused again and looked wearily to the south, calculating where the Germans might be waiting. "Who knows but that he might be the only one of us who actually survives this war."

THREE

Ten minutes later, the young rebel stood and watched the train roll away, the wooden platform vibrating beneath his feet. He felt so isolated, so alone, surrounded by unfamiliar places and people he didn't recognize. He didn't know where to go. He didn't know who to talk to. He didn't have any idea where to even start.

One thought rolled around in his head. *I don't know who I am!*

He looked at his surroundings while shivering in the cold. The sun couldn't quite burn its way through the western edge of the silver sky, and he realized that darkness was not far away. The snow beneath his feet had been heavily packed, leaving a wet layer of blackened slush, and there was a tinge of oily smoke in the air. The platform was full of people who had come to meet the train, hoping desperately that it would take them away from the coming Russians. All of them had been beaten back, there being not an open foot of space on the train. Now they angrily mulled around, talking and complaining among themselves. He listened to their voices, hearing the fear and frustration. He studied their faces, seeing the hunger in their eyes. Most of them were women, with a few children mixed in. There were several old men, bent and awkward with age, and a few that were young but with serious injuries that would have precluded them from fighting anymore.

Seven years before, Gorndask had been a modest but thriving town constructed around a small industrial complex that built wagons and farm equipment to be sold throughout Eastern Europe. But as the threat of war became all too real, the factory had been converted to make ammunition and aircraft parts. This, of course, doomed it to a constant barrage of shelling from the Germans before they took control of the town, then a hundred nights of bombing from the Allies, then new rounds of shelling from the Russian army as it grew near. The evidence of the nearly constant assault was all around him. Hardly a single building in the downtown district had escaped damage. Many of them had been completely destroyed. The train station, once the grandest structure in the town, was missing two walls, the gray bricks lying in a heap around the base of the old building. Looking south, along the main road that stretched through town, the only thing he saw was devastation. Bombed-out buildings. Burned-out homes. Stores that were missing every window. Streets pocked with craters and debris. Piles of shattered wood. Broken furniture. Charred automobiles. A few people wandered among the wreckage, searching for anything to burn, eat, or wear.

To his right, at the corner of a large intersection, a once beautiful rock home looked like it had nearly been blown in two. The grand staircase hung suspended in midair, ending abruptly six feet above the floor. A group of small children huddled underneath the staircase. Looking at them, he caught an unfamiliar sound, and he cocked his head to listen. Yes, there it was again. The children were laughing. They were laughing! He couldn't help but smile. And then he realized that there were other subtle but determined signs of rebuilding. A couple of horse-drawn trailers were being loaded with debris in an attempt to clear the streets, and a dozen open fires were burning, people warming themselves around the flames. He shifted his feet, turning slightly to his right. Near the main door that led into the terminal, a small pine tree had been decorated with red balls and silver tinsel, the slightest hint of Christmas cheer.

At that moment he felt a sudden sense of pride. He didn't know if this was his hometown, but he knew these were his people. And the war had not defeated them. They had not lost their desire to live, to reclaim some of the things that had been taken from them.

The old man watched him from the corner of the platform. He was small and bent, his hair thin and white around his red head, and his face was tight, his lips pinched around brown teeth.

His name was Zarek. Like some others, he had made a decision many years before. He wouldn't question. He wouldn't wonder. There was no right or wrong. There was survival. That was all that mattered to him now.

He studied the young man with unblinking eyes. At first he hadn't been sure, but now he was certain. He scowled in anger. A rebel here in Gorndask. The colonel was going to be furious.

Zarek moved toward a windowless building and hid behind one of the crumbling walls. He kept an eye on the wounded rebel from the shadows, then mumbled to himself, "No friends for you, my young wolf. There are no friends for you here."

Shivering, the young man searched the faces all around him, looking for someone he might recognize, someone who was even a little bit familiar, or a single friendly face in the crowd, but all he saw was strangers who looked at him suspiciously. He moved toward the edge of the train platform and stepped into the street. The crowd seemed to part before him. He paused, looking left and then right, having no idea where to go.

Reaching into his jacket pocket, he pulled out the mud-streaked photograph and flattened it in his palm. It showed a man and his wife standing arm in arm. She had dark hair and high cheekbones. He was much taller, probably ten years older, and dressed in a military uniform. Infantry stripes stretched the length of his pant legs. A silver badge shone from the center of his officer's cap, bearing the number of a regiment from the First World War.

How do I know that? he wondered. Then his mind seemed to flash in shadows and lights. He saw wooden stairs. A sleeping cat tucked in a corner. A warm kitchen that smelled of baking bread. A woman's voice from somewhere behind him. And then the image was gone.

He closed his eyes, trying desperately to hang onto the memory, but there was nothing he could do. It had vanished as thin smoke in the wind.

Opening his eyes, he realized that he was shaking with frustration. Yet there was something else. Something good. Something that gave him a hint of hope. The flashing memories were becoming . . . how would he describe it . . . *gentler.* Less urgent. Like a movie slowing down. Yes, they were still far too fast, still indecipherable. But they were not so frustratingly impossible to remember or comprehend.

He rubbed his face, then looked down at the picture once again. The couple was standing in front of a white fence with a narrow gate. In the background, a simple home was nestled between tall trees. The mother was reaching down to hold a child's hand. The photograph showed the hand and most of the child's arm, but there it was torn.

He stared at it for the thousandth time.

"This *has* to be my mother and my father," he whispered to himself. "Those have to be my parents, and that little hand *has* to be my own."

He stared a bit longer, then folded the photograph carefully, returned it to his pocket, and started walking through the small town, heading south along the main road. He realized that things were even worse than they had looked from his position at the station. Dozens of women and young orphans were camped in the shelled-out buildings. Many were simply living on the streets, the buildings too unstable and dangerous to enter safely anymore. Most of the people stared at him in confusion as he walked by. Many were apprehensive. All of them were curious. The bombing, the fleeing Nazis, the coming Russians, all of it had taken Gorndask's men and thrown them into the grinding gears of war. The sight of a young and apparently uninjured man demanded an explanation.

He looked apprehensively to the east. He knew the brutal Russian army was just a few days away. Soon, Russian T-52 tanks and heavy armor would be rolling through these streets.

How do I know that? he wondered again. He didn't know how he knew it, but he was certain. Just like he was certain that he knew how to shoot a rifle, work with dynamite, and apply first aid to a wounded man. He knew how to navigate with the stars, read a map, and drive a military truck. He knew how to swim a hundred feet underwater, make a land mine out of petroleum and nails, and throw a knife. He knew how to do these and many other things.

But he didn't know who he was.

The sun was setting now, and it was getting colder. Pulling up his jacket collar, he thought of the approaching army.

That was the reason the Polish people were hated by both the Russians and the Nazis. They were far too independent, far too freedom-loving. Like the Nazis, the Russians were bent on breaking their will.

He blew into his hands and started walking toward a broken church at the center of the town. Passing a burned-out building, he saw the girl out of the corner of his eye. Turning to look at her, he came to a stop. She couldn't have been more than eight or nine years old. She had dark, curly hair and enormous brown eyes. Her little face was dirty, her clothes in tatters, and she didn't even have a coat. Her little brother sat beside her. Same dark hair. Same dark eyes. Both of them were pale and thin; hunger and desperation cast a shadow across their faces. She held out her hands, begging for something to eat. "Please," she pleaded and pointed to her tummy. The little boy followed him expectantly with his eyes. "Please *pan,*" she repeated. "We are hungry."

When he didn't walk away, she struggled to her feet and moved toward him but came to a stop a safe distance away. She waited, every muscle tense, ready to spring back. She had learned that for every stranger who would help them, another three were just as likely to cause them harm. And she had seen what harm could come to children, things her little brother could not see. So she waited at the top of a pile of broken bricks, ready to grab his hand and run.

Looking at them, the man took a breath, his chest heaving with despair. She was so young. So desperate and yet so beautiful. How many children, how much beauty, how much virtue had been destroyed in this war.

He shook his head. "I'm sorry," he said, his hands extended. He forced a weak smile, then turned away and kept on walking.

He heard her sniffle with disappointment, but he didn't turn back. They weren't the only orphans begging on the streets. They weren't the only children who would die during the coming winter. There were far too many to be numbered–far too many for him to help. And he was done. His fight was over. There was nothing he could do.

Zarek watched the rebel walk down the blackened street. He hesitated a moment, then turned and hustled toward the back of the railroad station.

The sun would be setting soon, and it was just starting to snow again. Zarek pulled his dirty jacket up around his ears. Winter had fallen hard. It was going to be a cold night.

FOUR

SCHUTZSTAFFEL HEADQUARTERS BUILDING
THREE MILES OUTSIDE OF GORNDASK

It was a beautiful estate, huge by any measure, with rock walls, iron-domed chimneys, and a circular cobblestone drive. Owned by a former Polish leader of the Parliament—he and his family now dead—the estate had fallen into disrepair and was showing the stress of the German occupation.

Positioned on four hundred hectares a few miles from the outskirts of town, the estate now housed the vicious SS officers who had dedicated themselves to the cleansing of Poland. But the Allies didn't know that and couldn't have done anything about it anyway, it being impossible to target such a small building with the B-17s that had filled the sky.

The library was on the ground floor, just off the main entrance. It was a beautiful room, or at least it had been once, with wood floors, rosewood paneled walls, and heavy drapes over the arched windows. A large fireplace burned oversized logs, making the space uncomfortably warm. But the room was almost empty except for a table, a single chair, and a silver tray holding uneaten food.

The SS colonel stood by the fireplace and stared into the flames. He wore a uniform that was no longer authorized, all black with bloused leggings and high boots. It was perfectly pressed, and the silver ϟϟ on his lapel shone in the yellow light of the fire. A death's head badge was pinned in the middle of his cap, which was resting on the mantel. He was of average build, with an average face and dark hair, slicked back. The only thing remarkable about him were his eyes: close together, deeply set, intense, and deadly black.

He kept his head down, deep in thought. He seemed defeated. Tired. Someplace far away. He stared at a small, worn notebook in his hand, took a breath, tore out a single page, looked at the names that had been scrawled across the dirty paper, then tossed it into the fire. He watched the paper burn, then took another page, tore it out, read the names, tossed it into the fire.

His command sergeant, Sergeant Fisser, appeared through the double doors behind him. He was a tall man with dark features, a square jaw, and black stubble for hair. He moved into the room with brisk steps. "Colonel Müller, the men are ready, sir."

Müller stared at his notebook without responding. There were only a few pages left. He straightened up, shoved the notebook into his pocket, and nodded to Fisser.

Both men turned and walked toward the door.

FIVE

Zarek stood outside the pitiful hut looking through the single window. Though it was barely dusk, she had the gas lantern burning, and he fumed a bit, knowing they would soon be out of fuel. No fuel, no light, no heat—and so many winter nights ahead. Thinking on it, he realized it was nearly winter solstice. The sun was about to tip back to the south, causing the days to start growing a little longer.

He looked at the gloom around him, then turned east, toward the approaching Russians, and wondered if any of the people of his town would live to see the spring.

He listened carefully, tilting his head just a bit. Even his old ears could pick up the sound of artillery in the distance. Deep. Deadly. It rolled across the frozen landscape like distant thunder. He'd been told that the Russians had crossed the highway, the Germans' last line of defense. That meant he was about to get a new master. All of them were.

He shivered, then turned back to his hut, opened the door, and walked in.

The one-room shanty was clean but nearly empty. Bare slat walls. Bare wood floor. The only furniture consisted of a wood-burning stove, a rickety table, and three wood chairs. Two straw mattresses were in one corner. There was a sink below the window, but no running water. A small cabinet held wooden plates.

His daughter was knitting at the table, her sightless eyes staring straight ahead. She concentrated on her work, her fingers moving quickly across the scratchy yarn. A toddler was sitting on the wood floor beside her, content to play with rags that had been folded into the form of two dolls.

Zarek instantly brightened at the sight of the little girl. She looked up and squealed, "Grandpa!" Standing, she ran to him, holding out her arms. He caught her up and tossed her in the air. She laughed and he threw her in the air again, catching her gently and then holding her in his arms. The blind woman listened to the sound of her daughter's happy cries and smiled.

"How are you, *dzeiko?*" Zarek asked as he pulled the little girl close, smelling the softness of her skin.

The child leaned back and held out her hands as if asking. Zarek reached into his jacket and pulled out a block of goat cheese wrapped in brown paper. The little girl coaxed for it hungrily. Zarek unwrapped the light brown cheese and broke her off a piece.

His daughter took a deep breath, taking in the poignant smell. "Goat cheese, Father! Where did you get that? It smells delicious!"

Zarek moved toward the wooden cabinet beside the stove and searched through its contents. Salt. A few other spices. Matches. A couple of wooden plates. A small box of dry crackers. A glass container of olive oil. He took the crackers and oil, moved to sit at the table, pulled out a knife from his front pocket, and started cutting slices of the cheese. "Haven't I always taken care of you?" he answered.

"You always have, Father."

She reached blindly, knowing where he was by the sound of his work. He leaned over and took her hand, giving it a squeeze. The little girl tugged at him, and he lifted her to his lap, giving her another piece of cheese atop a cracker. "What would we do without you?" his daughter asked.

Zarek stopped cutting and glanced anxiously toward the front door. "You would starve, I suppose," he answered.

His daughter laughed. "You don't have to put it so bluntly."

"I'm sorry. A poor attempt at humor."

He put his granddaughter on the floor, reached across the table, and picked up the knitting from his daughter's lap. Holding it up to the light, he examined it very closely. The colors were mismatched and crooked, the ends frayed and out of place. "This is beautiful," he said.

"Is it? I'm so glad to hear you say that. It feels okay, but I can never really tell."

Zarek placed it back in her lap and she started to finger along the edge, searching for the loose end.

"It's very nice," Zarek assured her.

"Will it fetch a fair price?"

"When you're finished, I'll take it to the market and we'll see."

She reached out for his hand again. "You haven't taken off your coat," she said. Her voice was worried now. "Are you going out again tonight?"

Zarek swiped a cracker through the oil. "I won't be gone long." His voice was tense. He didn't want to have this conversation.

"Don't go, Father. Don't leave us tonight. The artillery is so close. It's getting closer! Why must you go?"

"Because I have to feed you."

His daughter frowned but didn't answer. The child fussed at his feet again, and Zarek reached down to pick her up.

The blind girl took another breath. "I can smell the cheese. It seems to fill the whole house."

He glanced at his nearly bare surroundings. "There's not much else to fill it," he said. He looked down and tickled the little girl under her chin. "But there's enough. You're enough to fill the emptiness, aren't you, my little *dzeiko.*"

The little girl reached out for his cracker and pulled it to her mouth.

"Is there . . . is there enough for me?" his daughter asked.

"Of course. Did you think I would forget you?"

He reached out and guided her hand toward the plate piled with the cheese and crackers. She felt the food and smiled. Zarek lifted another piece of cheese to his mouth but stopped when she suddenly pulled her hand back.

"Will you say grace for us, Father?"

Zarek put his cheese down. "Of course," he said.

SIX

He walked a couple of hundred yards, picking through rubble while working his way south toward a gray steeple standing over a partially damaged rock-and-mortar church. The first person he came to was an old woman dressed in a black dress, gray apron, and heavy combat boots laced ridiculously around her feet. He approached her with bleary eyes and an uncertain face, the pain in his head making him dizzy as he leaned down to speak. "Pardon," he said in a low voice, "I'm looking for someone." She stared up at him without emotion. He pulled out the picture and unfolded it for her to see. "Do you know these people?"

She glanced at the picture, then shook her head and turned away. He touched her arm and extended the picture toward her again. "Please, they are my parents."

She lifted an eyebrow and tilted her head, seeming to motion to the chaos all around them. "Do you really think that anyone is going to be able to help you?"

"You can't see it, but that's me holding my mother's hand. But I don't know . . ." He paused, completely speechless. "So many people have been killed . . ." His voice trailed off.

"They certainly have," she said sarcastically. She'd had a hundred such conversations over the past seven years. "All right," she finally sniffed while nodding toward the picture. "Where do they live?"

"I don't know."

"You don't know where your parents live?" She sounded suspicious now.

He hesitated, unsure of what to say. "I was injured . . ." How could he begin to explain? He could hardly even admit it to himself. *I don't know where my parents live. I don't know their names. I don't know who they are because I don't know who I am.*

She studied him, taking in the young face and soft eyes. She saw the pain there and felt a wave of sympathy. Turning to the picture, she lifted a finger and traced it along the woman's face. He waited anxiously, almost holding his breath, until she lifted her eyes. "I'm sorry," she said sadly. She wasn't speaking of the picture but of the fact that he, like all of them, had lost someone he loved. She patted his arm, turned, and moved on her way. He watched her go, then started walking toward the church again.

He passed a couple of older men, stopping to show them the picture. One of them demanded his gloves; the other asked him for a cigarette. Neither of them were any help. He walked toward a group of children, but they ran away as he approached. He found himself in the middle of the town. Broken cobblestone streets. Piles of rubble. Buildings blown into pieces. A few stores miraculously unharmed. A north and south road came together around a fountain, and the cobblestone streets were wide enough to form a small square. A church with rock spires looked down on the fountain where a statue lay facedown in two inches of dirty ice.

He walked toward a group of people who were standing around a small fire built in a large metal drum. It was a mixed group: a few men, a few children, a lot of older women. Most of them stood with bare hands extended toward the flames. Some didn't have coats, and he felt a surge of guilt for the jacket he was wearing. The shadows were growing deep, and a soft snow started falling, wetting his hair and melting on his face. He looked up, but the overcast was soaking up the last of the light. The church was on the corner across from the fire pit, and he heard a group of scraggly voices singing a Christmas carol.

Hearing the music, he froze, his lips pressed. His mind tumbled suddenly, seeming to flash in fragmented memories: *Explosions. Crying voices. Crawling along the ground. Running through a grove of burning trees.*

All of it fell upon him in a crushing weight of sadness that almost drove him to his knees. He bent over, his hands at his head, his eyes closed in pain.

She watched him from the second floor of the church. She was standing behind an oval window that looked out on the street, one of the few unbroken pieces of glass within a hundred miles. The window was covered in oily smudge, and she lifted a hand to clean off a small circle in front of her face.

She was startlingly beautiful, with dark hair, green eyes, and skin as smooth as silk. A strong eastern chin and high cheekbones gave a dignity to her face. She wore a white dress underneath a light blue apron, but both of them were filthy from the dirt and work of war. A silver necklace hung around her neck, a small pendant pressed against the skin between her collarbones. As she stared out through the window, a choir in the sanctuary started lifting their voices into the air.

She leaned her head against the brick window frame. Thin lines of decorative copper had been soldered into the tinted glass in an intricate design of the stars and the moon, and she absently traced her finger along the copper while watching him. He stood by the fire, silent, his hands stuffed into his pockets. As the choir started singing, he suddenly looked away, his eyes unfocused, as if he were entirely somewhere else. He was completely motionless for several long moments; then he seemed to stumble, bending as if in pain.

She watched him intently, her head resting against the brick, her eyes soft and wide.

Sadness. That was the only thing he felt, deep as his bones, nothing but sadness and despair. The sound of the choir seemed to penetrate his jumbled memories, and he turned toward the church, shaking his head. In the midst of all this darkness, the music seemed ridiculously out of place.

Then suddenly he stopped.

Did I ever believe? he wondered. Tilting his head, he stared absently across the square at the bombed-out church. But how could anyone believe? All you had to do was take a look around to know that even if there was a God, he didn't care about this people or this place!

He thought on that a moment, the choir voices coming and going in the soft wind. It was a slow song, haunting and powerful—an old Austrian Christmas hymn. He caught his breath. *An Austrian Christmas song!* And he knew all the words.

Still, still, still,
Weil's Kindlein schlafen will.
Die Englein tun schön jubilieren,
Bei dem Kripplein musizieren.

He *must* have learned that somewhere. Sometime and somewhere, he'd been taught to believe.

Still, still, still,
'Cause baby wants to sleep.
The angels jubilate beautifully,
By the manger making music.

The music ended and he moved a little closer to the fire. Silence filled the darkness. The crowd around him didn't speak.

He thought, *I can break down and reassemble a Błyskawica submachine gun in less than sixty seconds. I know that it was designed by Waclaw Zawrotny specifically for the Polish resistance. I know that it was assembled with screws instead of welds so that we could repair our own weapons. I remember all of this, but I don't know if I believe in God.*

She leaned toward the window, studying his face in the yellow light of the fire. She could see the strain in his eyes, the hurt and confusion. She could see the sag of his shoulders and the uncertain gesture of his hands.

He was lost and nearly broken and without a single friend.

"But the children could save you," she whispered to herself.

For a long time he didn't say anything, content to feel the heat of the fire. He realized that he was very hungry, but he had no idea where he would get anything to eat. A young girl standing beside her mother seemed to read his mind. "I'm hungry," she whimpered as she wrapped her arms around her mother's knee. The mother reached down and put her hand atop her head. *"Bog zapewni,"* she said. God will provide.

He glanced at the destruction all around him and shook his head in doubt.

The light snow had stopped, leaving a new dusting on the ground, and he wiped his head to press the moisture from his hair. A drop of melted snow rolled down his forehead and into his eye. One of the women watched him. "Where you from?" she asked.

He looked up. "I have no idea," he said.

The small group watched him, waiting for him to explain, but he didn't, so they went back to staring into the flames.

SEVEN

TWELVE MILES WEST OF GORNDASK

The sky was gray and growing darker, but the snow had stopped, leaving fresh powder atop the uneven ground, the trees drooping under its constant weight. The forest was thick on the south side of the track, with fields to the north, barren, snow-draped, and cold. A flock of black birds circled overhead, something tempting them from the edge of the forest. They hung in the sky, a tang of acid from hundreds of artillery and mortar explosions drifting in the wind.

The refugee train had come to a stop. The engine was no longer belching black smoke, but wisps of steam still hissed from the brake lines. The body of the engineer hung out of the engine window, both arms hanging limply toward the ground, his face leaning against the cold metal.

The refugees were standing in the snow, huddled close together. Children cried in fear and hunger. Mothers held them close. The SS officers, accompanied by a squad of regular army infantry, worked their way from car to car, pushing and screaming to get the last of the refugees off the train.

In the last car, the Devil's Rebels stood in a semicircle against the back wall, their faces drawn and resolved. One of them pulled at the bars on the windows, but he only gave it a half effort, knowing there was nothing he could do. There were at least a hundred German soldiers waiting for them outside the train, leaving no hope of escape.

What will we tell our children?

That we fought beside our brothers.

Like their brothers before them, they knew their fight for freedom was about to come to an end.

Colonel Müller stood on a small hill watching the soldiers work. He would have preferred to have only *Schutzstaffel* men under his command, but that was no longer possible. The war had thinned their ranks, leaving him a hundred regulars to carry out his work. He didn't know yet if he could trust the regular army soldiers, but he was about to find out.

He looked at the sky, checked his watch, then lit a cigarette. His command sergeant stood beside him, a black machine gun in his hand.

"How many?" Müller asked as he pulled a drag on the unfiltered smoke. He held his breath a moment, then exhaled through his nose. His dark eyes burned, black coals of resentment smoldering under heavy lids.

Fisser nodded toward the last car. "We were told there were more than a dozen."

Müller frowned. That would leave some stragglers. Completely unacceptable. He wanted this over with.

He glanced down at the dirty notebook in his hand, flipping

through the few remaining pages, then pulled out a stubby pencil and lifted his eyes to watch again.

It took twenty minutes to empty the train, contain the refugees inside a guarded circle, and round the rebels up. Müller watched and smoked, impatiently checking his watch and the darkening sky. Nineteen rebels were lined up outside the last car and pushed to their knees, the SS men standing guard. Satisfied that all was ready, Müller moved forward, his black boots leaving tracks in the fresh snow.

He came to a stop in front of the pitiful rebel soldiers. They kept their heads down. He stared at them as if he expected some kind of response. But they knew that they were going to die here, and there was nothing for them to say.

"Gentlemen, look at me," Müller finally said.

The rebels slowly looked up. Young and dirty faces. Anger. Resignation. One of them laughed, the high-pitched tone giving away his fear.

Müller moved forward, coming to a stop in front of the first rebel. "Urbanski," he said.

The rebel's face showed surprise.

Müller wrote his name in his little notebook, then moved to the next man. "Bobka," he said and then wrote. He worked his way down the line. He knew every man.

Finished, Müller nodded toward a young lieutenant who commanded the regulars, then turned and walked away. He heard a few sobs of fear behind him and then shots. He counted as he walked. The last shot was fired. Silence settled over the winter landscape. He stopped and turned toward Sergeant Fisser, who was following a few steps behind. "The others too," he said in a low voice.

Fisser hesitated, glancing back toward the huddled refugees, then turned and started walking back.

EIGHT

The young rebel stood by the fire. As time passed, the night grew colder. One by one the villagers peeled away, leaving for their bombed-out homes or hovels or wherever they were going to sleep. A few of them said good night, but most turned and left without a word. He stood alone until the embers had turned to coals and gray ash. The night was perfectly quiet: cold and still, black and empty as the space between the stars.

He heard the shuffling behind him and quickly turned, his right hand moving instinctively toward his hip as if reaching for a weapon. A man was hobbling toward him with the help of a makeshift crutch. The stranger looked to be about thirty, maybe a little older. His face was tense beneath a light beard and brown hair, and his eyes were always moving, darting anxiously here and there. He wore a mix of civilian and military clothing: thick cotton farmer pants, leather combat boots, a white shirt underneath a heavy military coat. His left leg was missing from just above the knee and he limped along on a crutch made from a branch of gnarled oak, the knotty top worn smooth as glass. He moved toward the fire, seemingly disappointed at the dying coals.

"So cold," he said.

The rebel threw on a couple of logs and stirred the embers, making the fire leap into an orange and yellow flame. The stranger moved closer and extended his hands, then nodded to introduce himself. "Antoni Geric," he said.

The younger man nodded back but only grunted. Both of them were silent for a moment. Finally the rebel asked, "When were you injured?"

Antoni seemed to calculate. "Funny. It's my anniversary. Two years ago today. Outside of Stalingrad."

The rebel nodded sympathetically. "Stalingrad. A hard place."

The wounded man pulled out a wooden pipe, tapped it over his open palm, and shoved it in his mouth. He didn't have any tobacco, but he still sucked on the mouthpiece as he thought. "I was conscripted when the Germans ran us through in thirty-nine. They took me and my two brothers. I was sixteen years old. My older brother was seventeen; my little brother two years younger than me."

The young rebel glanced at him out of the corner of his eye. The war had aged the man many years. Behind them, from some unseen shelter, they could hear a baby cry.

Antoni put his empty pipe back into his pocket and smiled bitterly. "I should be famous, you know. I have the unlikely distinction of having fought on not one, and not two, but on three different sides of this war. I fought for the Germans, and then the Russians, and then . . ." he paused and looked at the younger man carefully ". . . and then I fought with the rebels. Now, *that's* the good side of the war."

The younger man looked away. This was very dangerous ground.

Antoni lowered his voice and used his crutch to move a couple of steps toward him. "I was first conscripted by the Germans when they invaded. We had no choice, of course. Everyone they didn't kill, they forced into their army. Fodder for the enemy. Targets to take the bullets before they sent their own men in. They gave me five days training and sent me into the fight. Some of us didn't even have a weapon. We were attacking with rocks and sticks. Such is what the Germans thought of us. From there I was sent east to the Baltics. Kiev. Western Russia. My unit spent the winter outside of Stalingrad. Tens of thousands of us died. After nearly freezing to death or starving to death, take your pick, we were taken captive by the Russians. Turns out there are exactly two things worse than death. Fighting for the Germans is the first one. Being captured by the Russians is the second."

The crying child in the darkness fell silent and the night was still. The pipe came out again and he sucked it as they studied each other in the light of the yellow flames. Antoni used his crutch to push a rusted ten-gallon bucket a little closer to the fire and sat down. "It didn't take Stalin five minutes to find a use for us Polish prisoners. He granted us amnesty—for what crime, I don't know—and sent us back into the war, but this time for the Bolsheviks. We Poles are good fighters, not something either side is willing to waste. But once the leg was gone, I was left to my own doings. Took me eight months to beg and crawl my way back home."

Antoni stared into the fire. "It's a hell of a thing," he whispered. "I crawled a thousand miles out of Russia, and now here they are again, knocking at my door. Germans to the west. Warsaw will fall in the next few days. I hear that entire city looks like this." He motioned to the devastation all around him. "Ninety percent of the city is destroyed. Beautiful Warsaw, the city that used to be my home. The Germans are having mass executions, killing thousands every day. And why do they do this? Because we are Polish. So instead we wait here for the Russians, who have killed a million of us already. And why do they kill us? Because we are Polish." He sucked on his pipe, drawing air into his mouth. "God hates the Jews, the gypsies, and the Poles, it seems."

The younger man shook his head. "I don't believe that."

"How could you not?"

"Because there is no God to hate or love us," he said. "If there was a God, we wouldn't be surrounded by starving children, smoldering churches, and old women scavenging for food." He motioned to Antoni. "If there was a God, then you would have both legs."

Antoni pressed his lips together and shrugged. "Maybe. But I think there has to be another answer. At least I hope there is."

The younger man looked away. "So you were saying about the rebels?" he asked carefully.

"*Tak*. But you know as much about that as I do."

Antoni was silent as the other man stared at him. A long moment passed. "So that's the way it is," Antoni finally said.

One of the logs shifted on the fire, and a burst of glowing ash lifted on the heat, a dozen red embers rising into the air. Both of them lifted their faces to watch them until they cooled enough to turn dark and float back to the earth like black snowflakes. Antoni turned to look at the rebel, then leaned forward. Reaching underneath his coat, he pulled out a handgun and threw it to him. The rebel caught it expertly, turned it in his hand, cycled the action, and pointed it at Antoni, ready to shoot.

"I heard you were pretty good with that thing," Antoni said.

The rebel sighted down the barrel. "I can hit out to one hundred sixty meters, if the winds are calm."

Antoni snorted. "No one can do that with a handgun."

"I can."

Antoni snorted again. "I was with Gorky and the Southerns, so we didn't fight together, but I recognize your face. And if I know you, then Colonel Müller will know you too. It's foolish to be out here, walking among our people. You put the entire town in danger. They will come looking, and if they don't find you, these people will pay the price."

Everything Antoni said only added to his confusion, but something in the words and the dreadful way he said them made his gut tighten up.

Antoni rubbed his hands through his hair, frustration growing on his face. "I saw you get off the train. A lot of people did." He stopped and waited. The younger man stared blankly. "You don't know what happened to the train, do you?" Antoni continued. "No. Of course. How could you know? The Germans interdicted it just an hour out of town. They dragged all the passengers off. When they found the rebels, they killed everyone on the train. Every single person. That is what we are up against. That is what we face.

"They're looking for us," the wounded man concluded in a defiant voice. "And they're not satisfied to just beat us, they have to destroy us, every one. It makes no sense, I know that, but very little does. Why are they still sending trainloads of Jews to the camps? Why are they committing valuable men and equipment to relocation and cleansing efforts when they are losing the war? The same logic applies to us. It doesn't matter if they find themselves in defeat, the Nazis will do whatever it takes to see each and every one of us killed.

"So go wherever you are going to go, but do it quickly and in the darkness. You make things very dangerous for our countrymen if you are seen."

The younger man nodded. "*Tak.*"

They stood a few more minutes. The fire was dying now, leaving glowing embers in the middle of the pit. "We can't be seen together," the wounded man said. "It's much too dangerous. I'm going north. And you are . . . ?"

The rebel shrugged. "I might stay here."

Antoni frowned. "Do whatever you see as right," he said, then turned to leave. He had hobbled only a few steps away when he turned back. "I have a family," he said. "Crazy, I know, a cripple like me, but I have a wife and she is beautiful and she doesn't seem to care about my leg."

The other man was silent.

"I even have a little girl."

"I'm sure that she is beautiful as well."

"You have no idea how beautiful she is. God gave me this great gift, and I don't want to lose it. The war is over. I've done everything that I could do. *We've* done everything we could do. All I want is to see my family. I just want to go home."

"I hope you make it."

"I will," Antoni said. He lifted his hand to wave good-bye. "Good luck, Lucas," he said.

And with those words, the rebel's world suddenly shifted on its poles, spinning on its axis like a ball spinning through the air. His mind flashed back, the memories coming in lightning-quick images of emotions and sounds and smells. They ran through his head with a force that made him close his eyes to the flashing in his head. *A yellow-painted hallway. A woman's voice calling from the bottom of a curved stairway. A black dog. A sun-drenched sky. His mother walking toward him across a wide lawn. He saw her face. He heard her speaking. "Lucas, I'm going to miss you . . ."*

Lucas. His name was Lucas!

"I pray that God will bless you. You know I love you, Lucas . . ."

He seemed to falter, almost bending at his knees. Antoni watched him, reaching out a hand as if to brace him.

Lucas stared at him and smiled. *My name is Lucas Capek.* He wanted to weep with joy.

NINE

He stood by the fire long after Antoni had left. It seemed a great victory, knowing his name, and he savored the feeling though it also brought frustration that the revelations had stopped there.

How long would it take, he wondered, before he remembered the rest of his life?

Looking around, he realized that the streets were deserted, everyone too cold and hungry to be out any longer. The fire had burned down and the night was very dark, with only a few flickering lights glowing from the windows of the church. Shivering, he turned and walked toward it. He was suddenly exhausted. All he wanted was to sleep.

The stone church had generally been spared from destruction, though most of the windows were broken and the north spire was completely blown away. It was set back only a few feet from the cobblestone street, and the heavy wooden door was not locked. He carefully pushed the door back, expecting to find other refugees inside, and was surprised to see the sanctum empty. It was noticeably warmer in the church, and the interior was dimly lit by candles in the windows on both sides of the altar.

Turning to shut the door, he saw her sitting in the shadows on the back pew. Her head was bowed, as if in prayer, and she raised her eyes reluctantly at the sound of the door moving on its metal hinges.

He looked at her curiously. White dress. Light blue apron. Canvas shoes. Dark hair. Light skin. Her clothes were war-dirty, but her face and hands were clean. She was beautiful in the candle-light, and he blurted out without thinking, "What are you doing here?"

She looked at him curiously but didn't answer.

He blushed, embarrassed. "I didn't mean that the way it sounded," he stumbled to explain. "It sounded . . . something like I didn't mean it to. It's just that, I don't know, you seem a little out of place."

She smiled, her eyes sparkling in the flickering light. He studied her carefully. At first he thought that she was beautiful, but then he realized that wasn't right. She wasn't beautiful, it was more like . . . elegant, he supposed. And there was something else about her, something in her deliberate movements, in her calm reaction to his coming into the church. She showed no fear or hesitation. In a world of so much uncertainty, she was supremely confident.

He stood there awkwardly until she motioned to the front of the chapel. She stood and walked toward the rounded stone. Reaching underneath her apron, she pulled out two small loaves of bread and placed them on the altar. He watched her curiously.

"When we have extra, we leave it here for those who might need a little help," she explained.

He watched her skeptically, then glanced through the open

window to the devastation outside. "Are you sure you want to do that?"

"I do," she replied as she carefully positioned the loaves in the middle of the altar. Turning to face him, she motioned for him to come closer. He moved beside the flickering candles, his face barely illuminated by the yellow light.

"My name is Melina."

"Lucas," he offered simply. *Lucas! My name is Lucas!* Without knowing it, he smiled.

She watched him and gently laughed. "You seem very pleased at that."

"I'm sorry. It would be hard to explain."

"Is that your real name?" she asked suspiciously.

"It is."

She hesitated. "Are you from Gorndask?"

He stared at the stone floor and waited too long before he answered. "That's what they told me."

"That's a funny answer. You're either from here or you're not."

"Like I said, it would take a long time to explain."

She moved toward the nearest pew and sat, her face cast in shadows from the distant flame. He watched her carefully. Yes, indeed, she was *elegancki.*

"I know many people in town," she said. It seemed as if she were talking to herself, trying to put the pieces of a puzzle together. She shook her head in conclusion. "Are you sure this is your home?"

He suddenly felt homeless and alone. "If it's not, then I have nothing."

She watched his reaction and then smiled again. Even in his loneliness, he couldn't help but smile back.

"What about you?" he asked. "Are you from Gorndask?"

She shook her head. "I'm from somewhere else."

"Somewhere close?"

"Close enough to get here."

It was his turn to laugh a bit. "That seems a little evasive."

Melina smiled shyly. "It's a dangerous time. One must be careful."

"But you're alone?"

"No, I have a family."

Lucas motioned around the empty church. "But here you are . . . alone . . . at night . . ."

Melina stared away in thought. Lucas waited until she finally turned back to him. "My family has been scattered by the war."

"You and I are the same, then."

"You and I and ten million others," she said.

"It's not good to be alone. Like you said, it is a dangerous time. Much more dangerous for someone like yourself," Lucas warned.

"I'll be all right."

Lucas looked around the empty chapel, then stared through the broken windows to the darkness outside. "If you say so," he shrugged.

She smiled at him again. "You've created a bit of a stir here. A lot of people are wondering who you are, why you are here. They think you are one of the rebels, which makes it hard for them if that is true. It puts them in a hard place. So some of them don't trust you." She folded her arms as if she were suddenly cold, and the candles seemed to flare up, casting lively shadows across her face. "You seem the trusting kind. I don't want to ruin that, but you shouldn't trust, at least not everyone."

Lucas snorted. "Believe me, I know that people will disappoint you."

"It's just that people get hard when they're fighting to survive.

They lose a bit of their humanness when they think that they might die. A bit more when they are hungry. A bit more when they are cold. A lot more when they have children who are also cold and hungry. It doesn't mean that they're bad people, just that they've had a bad time. But you have to know the difference, and I'm not sure you do."

"I've seen enough to know the difference."

Melina thought a moment, then flipped her hands across her apron, hopelessly brushing at the dirt. She stopped and looked up at him. "I don't know if you do," she said.

"I don't think you know anything about me."

She looked away and nodded. "Of course not. Forgive me. How could I know?"

TEN

***SCHUTZSTAFFEL* HEADQUARTERS BUILDING**

THREE MILES OUTSIDE OF GORNDASK

Zarek limped toward the SS headquarters building, stumbling through the metal gate in the high stone wall that led to the rock mansion. Behind the gate, a rock path wound between two rows of large oak trees, their bare branches a thousand crooked fingers against the overcast sky. The snow had stopped, leaving a thin skiff of white clinging to every branch. The night was quiet, the shelling having stopped until morning, and the old man's halting footsteps were muffled by the fresh snow.

His heart was beating wildly in his chest. He'd seen the colonel kill for less than what he was about to tell him, and though he didn't have a lot to live for, he wanted desperately to live.

The large house was nestled fifty yards back from the gate. Rock arches loomed over every window. Soft yellow light shone from the gas lanterns illuminating the lower windows. But as with everything in Poland, the war had been hard on the mansion, and it desperately needed repairs. The paint was worn and peeling.

Broken red tiles clung to the roof. The shrubs were overgrown and bent beneath the weight of the snow.

Five minutes after knocking on the huge oak front door, Zarek was shown into the library. He stood alone, a frail and bent old man underneath the vaulted ceiling. The room was hot from a roaring fire in the fireplace. He savored the warmth. Time passed. He didn't move.

Taking a quick look around, he realized the library was much emptier than when he'd been here before. No more paintings. No more valuable porcelain vases or marble busts. Much of the beautiful leather furniture was gone as well. A half-eaten tray of food sat on a small table beside the only chair in the room. Looking at it, he felt his mouth start to water, thick saliva forming in the back of his throat. He was tempted to grab the food and stuff it in his coat pocket, but of course he didn't move.

Beside the silver tray of food, he noticed a silver-framed picture. He slowly bent over and focused on the photograph. Müller stood proudly beside another Nazi officer, his silver ϟϟ rank shining on his officer's cap. The commander of the *Schutzstaffel* stood beside him, Himmler's face all scowl, his shoulders drooping. Both men had their hands stuffed in the pockets of knee-length overcoats. It was overcast and muddy. Behind them was a brick wall, mangled strands of razor wire coiled along the top. To the right of the wall, a train of boxcars extended into the mist. Looking closely, Zarek could see human arms reaching out desperately between the slats of the cattle cars.

A handwritten inscription was scribbled across the photograph: LOYALTY AND HONOR.

The old man stared at the picture, squinting just a bit. Even though it was only a photograph, he could feel the evil, the cold and fear and pain.

He turned suddenly to see Colonel Müller standing beside him, and he stepped back in surprise. The colonel looked at him, then down at the photograph. Reaching across the old man's body, Müller took the photo and walked toward the fire. Glancing back, he tossed it into the flame.

"Why are you here?" he asked.

The old man quivered. "I saw one of the Devil's Rebels," he answered quickly.

The colonel scowled. He wore a black shirt with gray pants, and an SS Mauser C96 handgun was strapped to his leather belt. He stared at Zarek, then turned and started to walk away. "We killed all the rebels on the train," he said as he walked.

"No, sir. He got off the train this afternoon. I recognized him. I even know his name."

Müller stopped. He slowly turned around and stared at the old man, his eyes smoldering with rage.

"It was Lucas Capek," Zarek stammered. "The young man who—"

"I know who Capek is!" Müller snapped. "Are you certain it was him?"

Zarek gulped. "I am certain, sir."

The *Schutzstaffel* officer started moving around the room. It only took a moment before he was pacing in rage. "Why did he get off the train?"

"I don't know, sir."

"Was he injured?"

"No, sir, not that I could tell. A little blood on his face, but what is that in this war?"

Müller continued pacing. "Why did they let him off the train?" he demanded again.

"I don't know, sir. Maybe it was what you said before. They are disbanding. Running like rats before a fire."

The colonel snorted. "The Devils don't run. They are the most highly trained combatants the Poles have produced. German speakers. Expert snipers. Expert at demolition, infiltration, sabotage. Does that sound to you like the kind of fighter who would run?"

Zarek kept his head down and didn't answer.

The colonel swore bitterly. Of all of the enemies to the *Reich,* he considered the rebels the most despicable. Worse than the Jews. Worse than the horse-head Bolsheviks! Had any of his enemies caused any more damage to his *Vaterland* or more insult to the *Führer*?

"Where did he go?" he demanded.

"Sir," Zarek stammered, his voice thick with fear, "I lost him in the crowd. Then I came—"

"You don't know where he is!"

Zarek started choking. "Sir, I thought it best to come and tell you. I thought—"

"Shut up!" the colonel hissed as he stepped away from Zarek. He resumed pacing, deep in thought.

How to find the rebel? How to kill him?

At one time there had been ten thousand people in Gorndask, but there were fewer now, thousands of them dead already from the war. He would line them up and shoot them all if he had the time and the ammunition. But he didn't. Even if he couldn't kill them all, however, he had to find the last of the rebels. It would haunt him for the rest of his life to let any of them live.

He turned back to his cowering spy, one of the few men in the city who was willing to betray his countrymen for a block of cheese.

"What is the one thing you want, my Polish friend?" he asked tartly.

Zarek kept his head down. "To live, sir."

"That much we've established. And why do you want to live?"

"Sir, I have a family."

"Yes, that wretch of a family. A blind daughter. Her bastard daughter of a German traitor. Now, how long do you think they'll live without my protection and what I pay you?"

Zarek swallowed hard. "Sir, it is my greatest desire to never know."

"So what must you do now?"

"Find the rebel, sir."

"Yes. Find him so I can kill him. Now go."

ELEVEN

The night was quiet, cold, and dark as only winter nights can be in the middle of a war. The fighting would continue in the morning, but that was a few hours away yet.

Lucas moved to the altar and leaned against the white stone, the corners worn smooth as glass from five hundred years of worship. He didn't look at Melina but kept his eyes on the deep shadows in the corner of the sanctuary. Melina watched him, her face illuminated in the yellow candlelight.

"I've been told that you are looking for your family," she said, her voice soft as a whisper.

He reached into his pocket, pulled his picture out, and extended it toward her. She moved closer to the candles and held it up to the light.

"My parents," he explained. "The picture is torn, but that's me, holding my mother's hand when I was just a boy."

"When you were just a boy?" she said as if she were talking to herself. She studied it a long time, turning it from side to side to catch the best angle in the flickering light. Watching the intensity with which she looked at the picture, Lucas grew suddenly tense. He had expected her to glance at it quickly and then hand it back, but she hadn't. He felt his chest tighten, and he realized that he was holding his breath.

She finally turned to him, her almond eyes soft in the dim light. "I'm sorry," was all she said.

He looked away, lost in sadness. She watched him and then took a step toward him. "Lucas, do you even know if they're alive?" she asked him gently.

He took a breath, then dropped his head, staring at the floor in sudden anguish. He didn't answer. She waited. The sigh of the wind blowing through the shattered windows was the only sound. The candles flickered again and the shadows danced. The smell of smoky drapes and wet stone permeated the air. His face was darkened by the moving shadows.

"Lucas, do you really think they are alive?" Melina prodded.

His chin started to quiver, and he raised a hand to hide it. Inside, his heart was breaking.

"No . . . no . . . they're not alive," he whispered. "I don't know how I know that, but I know that they are dead."

They stood in silence. Lucas kept his eyes down as he slowly shook his head.

"I'm sorry," Melina said again. She watched him a long moment and then said, "I need to tell you something."

He didn't answer.

"There is a train leaving from Brzeg on Monday morning. Christmas Day. A refugee train. Very few know of its departure. It's going south, toward the American lines. It is your only hope for life, for freedom, your only chance of escape. If you stay here, you will die."

TWELVE

Colonel Müller stood by the fireplace, staring into the flames. His arms were crossed against his chest, and the firelight reflected in the darkness of his eyes. He looked tired but defiant. Angry and cruel. He reached into his pocket, pulled out the worn notebook, stared at it a moment, then shoved it back into his breast pocket and sat down in the single chair.

"Command Sergeant!" he called.

Sergeant Fisser immediately walked into the room. He wore the usual crisp combat uniform, with its black boots and bloused pants. But, unlike before, he carried a helmet underneath his arm and a rifle across his back. As he opened the door, the commotion of men at war could be heard from the hall.

"Sir," he answered wearily.

Müller motioned to the open door, and the sergeant pulled it closed. "You heard what our Polish friend told me?" he asked.

"I did, sir."

"And your thoughts?"

"I think, sir, that you would kill everyone in Gorndask if that's what it took to find this rebel."

Müller pressed his thin lips into a smile. His aide-de-camp knew him well. "Indeed, I've considered that already. But it's rather impractical, isn't it, Command Sergeant. Seven or eight thousand people. Seven or eight thousand rounds of ammunition. A week to round them up and kill them. I don't know if we have time."

The sergeant seemed to think. "They're doing it in Warsaw."

"But that's a long way from here. Many miles from the Russians. Their situation is not as urgent. They simply have more time."

Fisser nodded. "They do, sir." He glanced over his shoulder toward the French doors and the chaotic work that was going on throughout the headquarters building. "We have only a few days. Maybe less."

Müller lit a cigarette and sucked in a mouthful of smoke, then let it drift out, pulling it in through his nose again. He lifted the tray of food from the table and set it in his lap. Chicken legs and wings soaked in brown sauce and black pepper. He lifted a piece of meat and studied it.

"Let me ask you something, Command Sergeant. Of all of our enemies, who do you think is the most dangerous?"

Fisser hesitated. Müller took a single bite from a leg of chicken, chewed it slowly, then threw the rest of the meat into the fire.

"That is an interesting question, sir," Fisser said.

"Interesting? Or dangerous?" Müller lifted another chicken leg.

"Both, sir."

"But why would it be dangerous? The answer is so obvious. I see no threat in examining the question."

Fisser remained silent. Müller stared at the leg, took a single bite, threw the rest into the fire. "All right, let me rephrase the question. Who is the most dangerous of our enemies *to me?*"

Fisser knew immediately. "The rebels, sir, of course."

Müller picked up the last of piece of chicken, stared at it, and threw it into the fire without even taking a bite. "Yes, the rebel traitors. For you see, Command Sergeant, our *Führer,* our Master . . ." Müller caught himself and quickly pressed his lips together, then spit out the next words. "The . . . *Führer* gave me a task. So I'm going to kill the rebels. It will be my last mission. Then, as a final act of submission, I'll do what he commanded me to do but what I wouldn't do before."

THIRTEEN

The room was cracked and crumbling, the floor covered with pieces of shattered brick, patches of exposed wood and scorched plaster covering the walls. Though the battered home had been deserted, much of the furniture had been left behind. It had been pushed into one corner and was now covered in dirt and debris. The children huddled together on the worn couch, their arms around each other. A filthy blanket was tucked around their faces. The little boy's head was resting on his sister's shoulder. He took a deep breath and shivered in his sleep.

Melina walked through the front door, a small lantern in her hand. She quietly closed the door behind her, held the lamp up, and smiled at the little girl. "Hello, Cela," she whispered.

"Melina, what are you doing here?" The girl could barely contain the relief in her voice.

Melina nodded to her sleeping brother. "I don't want to wake him," she whispered as she walked toward the dusty table. She pulled out a loaf of bread and laid it there. Cela watched her expectantly.

"Why are you so good to us, Melina?"

"Because you need some help," the woman answered.

"You hardly know us. We're only strangers. And there are lots of children who need help."

Melina walked over and knelt beside the old couch. She reached out and brushed aside a strand of Cela's hair. "I had a little sister just like you. When I look at you and Aron . . . well, it just makes me want to help."

Cela leaned her head against her little brother. "Aron and I are glad you're here with us tonight."

Melina smiled. "I don't know if Aron really cares. I think that he's asleep."

Cela was already drifting off as well. Melina reached out and tucked the blanket up around her chin. "Go to sleep now," she whispered.

Cela closed her eyes. "Will you sing to us?" she mumbled through deep breaths.

Melina looked at the children, her head tilted to the side. Their frail bodies had obviously suffered from constant hunger, but they were beautiful children still. And they looked so much alike: the same unruly hair, the same dark skin, the same long eyelashes.

It was heartbreaking to watch them shiver from the cold.

Reaching down, Melina pushed aside another curl of Cela's wild hair. Then she knelt beside the children and held them close. She started singing gently, her voice soft but clear.

Little children you are mine now
Little children go to sleep
Little children I will watch you
From the gates of heaven's keep.

Little children you are mine now
In the darkness, there is fright
But little children you will find me
In the warmth of morning light.

So little children close your eyes now
Sleep on peaceful through the night
My angels' folded arms around you
Will keep you safe by heaven's might.

Her voice was barely above a whisper, but it seemed to fill the empty darkness. The children's breathing slowed, and they quit shivering as she held them in her arms.

FOURTEEN

The sun was barely up, its light filtering with a white haze that didn't have the energy to burn through the overcast. It was cold, the air wet and seemingly on the edge of snow. The streets were already full of people who were busy scavenging, cooking over fires, and talking in small groups here and there. Contradicting rumors were flying among the nervous villagers. "The Russians are just across the river," some said. "They are getting ready to bomb and mortar the town into smithereens. Why? Because we are Polish. What more reason do they need!"

"No, that can't be!" another answered. An entire battalion of German reinforcements had already attacked from the northern flank and were driving the Russians back, capturing and killing thousands of Slavic soldiers in a brutal counterattack.

Some said it was better to have the Nazis than the Russians, though many snorted at the thought.

No again, others answered, the war was stalled, both armies unable to gain any ground, with most of the fighting to the south.

Thousands of bodies were lying in the snow from the last twenty-four hours of fighting, which meant the townspeople would be forced, once again, to go out and bury them.

Among all the rumors, this much was clear: there was no hope for the city. One way or another, they were going to be bombed and shelled and occupied. There was no way to leave and nowhere to go. Better to stay here and suffer with your friends and family than to be caught by either army out on the road.

Then, sometime after sunrise, there came a sound beyond the pine-covered hills that belied all the rumors and speculation. The crash of heavy artillery impacting the frozen ground could be heard from the east. Everyone stopped and turned at the sound of the first rumble. Within minutes, there was a nearly constant roll of artillery echoing across the snowy terrain. It was an unearthly sound, shorter, deeper, and far more powerful than any natural storm.

But the frightening noise put all the rumors to rest. The lines of combat were at their door.

The inside of the chapel was cast in a pale light. Deep shadows filled the corners, and the wooden pews were cold and hard. Time passed, the mortars rumbled, and the sun continued to rise, but Lucas slept on, shivering underneath his jacket. Then he heard something different and was instantly awake. He jerked up, his eyes scanning wildly around the chapel as he reached for a weapon that was not there. He heard it again and cocked his head. Muffled by the overcast, it was so quiet that he felt it as much as heard it, a barely audible *clank* in his ear. He turned toward the sound. It was still far off, but getting closer. He unconsciously took a sudden breath.

He could tell immediately what it was. A *Sonderkraftfahrzeug,* or SdKfz 6 half-track. A long and gangly vehicle, with rubber tires in the front and metal tank tracks in the back, it could transport up to eleven men while pulling a 10.5 howitzer. But its small engine made it dangerously underpowered and lightly armored. The gas tanks were not protected, and even small arms were capable of penetrating and causing a fire or explosion.

How do I know this? he wondered for the first time that day.

It didn't matter. He knew it. And he knew they were coming toward the square, not more than a few blocks away.

He rolled over on the wooden pew and dropped onto the floor. He was cold and stiff and his head hurt as he began to crawl toward the narrow stairs that led to the second-floor balcony. He stayed low, not showing himself against the broken windows that ran the length of the chapel. Reaching the stairway, he crawled up the steps. At the back of the balcony there was a large oval window that looked out onto the city square. He moved toward it, then pressed himself against the brick wall and looked out. The window was smudged with oily soot, but he didn't wipe it away, afraid of exposing himself.

He didn't know it—and he would never know it—but he was standing exactly where Melina had stood the night before.

He peered cautiously through the dirty glass. Two SdKfz 6s were rolling down the street from the north, weaving among the rubble, their metal tracks clattering across the cobblestone street. From the south, two more SdKfz 6s were coming, their engines racing to reach the square at the same time as their companions. He shook his head in despair, knowing that people were about to die.

Lucas could see that each of the assault vehicles contained two drivers. Half a dozen German soldiers were in the open backs, all of them facing the villagers, their rifles ready. One vehicle stopped on each of the streets that led into the square, blocking any exit. The other two vehicles circled the damaged fountain, their soldiers carefully looking for any threat before they stopped. When they pulled up at last, the infantrymen jumped out and quickly set up a perimeter of self-protection, their faces intent and angry. Working in teams, the soldiers began to round the townspeople up, screaming and pushing and herding them together into the center of the square. A little boy stood grounded in fright, unable to move. The nearest soldier brought the butt of his rifle down on the back of the child's head, and he fell without moving. His mother screamed and ran toward him, but she was forced to join the others, crying and reaching for her child. A thin-faced colonel got out of the first vehicle and strode among the terrified citizens. Dark-eyed and quick, he was dressed in a full-length black leather coat, an eagle with outstretched talons glinting against the dark fabric of his officer's cap.

The citizens gasped as he emerged from the vehicle. *Schutzstaffel.* An SS officer! Dedicated to the purification of the Fatherland. Held by blood oaths to maintain absolute obedience to the *Führer.* With the blood of more than twelve million innocent people on their hands, their enemies were the Jews and Bolsheviks—and certainly the Poles.

The villagers of Gorndask hardly dared to look at him as a hush of terror fell among them.

Lucas turned desperately from the window. His eyes moved around the church, searching for any kind of weapon. A blackened shovel against the coal chute. A metal poker near the ancient fireplace. A heavy broom in the corner. What were any of these against fifty armed men?

He glanced at the back of the chapel, noting the door behind the altar. A way to escape! A place to hide! But he didn't want to run. He wanted to fight!

"I need a weapon!" he hissed. Then he suddenly stopped.

He knew where he could get one.

The colonel nodded to his command sergeant, who barked at the terrified crowd. "You are harboring a rebel," Fisser shouted. "Tell us where he is and we will let you live!"

No one spoke.

The Germans selected five old men and lined them up, forced them to their knees, and pushed their faces down.

"If you allow the Devils to stray among you, then you will pay the price," Fisser shouted. "The choice is yours. Give us what we want and you live. Betray us and you will die."

A murmur of confusion began to sweep through the terrified crowd. An old man stepped forward. "We have no rebels. I swear, we would tell you if we knew!"

Fisser scowled in disgust. "I ask you for the last time . . ."

The crowd fell into silence. "We would tell you," a women's voice cried desperately from the back.

Fisser turned and looked at Müller. The colonel stared at the crowd, rage and blackness in his eyes. He took a slow drag on his cigarette, stared at the burning ember, picked a piece of tobacco from the tip of his tongue, then nodded to Fisser.

Five shots rang out in near unison. The men fell lifeless onto the snowy ground, their warm blood flowing underneath them. It melted the thin layer of snow as it spread, exposing the frozen ground beneath their faces and half-open eyes. The villagers screamed and huddled even closer together. Some of the women turned away from the carnage. A few of the older ones stared in shock. Some didn't react at all, having seen much worse.

Müller glanced down at his watch, impatient that it was taking so much time.

"You will tell us," Fisser shouted at the crowd.

The villagers huddled, not knowing what to do. The colonel studied them, furious at their insolence, then motioned to his sergeant once again.

"Five more," he said.

Lucas crawled across the floor, getting away from the window, then ran down the stairs. Running up the aisle of the chapel, he grabbed one of the window draperies and jerked it down. The heavy cloth fell into his hands, musty and deep purple. Stopping at the coal chute, he bent and pulled the door open. The sides of the chute were coated in black dust. He rubbed his hands through it until they were black, then rubbed it on his face, his teeth, his hair. Taking off his boots, he rubbed his feet as well. He threw the drapery over his head and shoulders, pulling it tight against his neck, leaving only his dirty face exposed. Bending over, he started shuffling toward the door. The transformation was dramatic. He had become a filthy beggar, shoeless and dirty faced, too crippled to even stand. With his black face barely exposed, he could have been twenty or eighty; it was impossible to tell.

Stepping outside, he hurried to the street. One of the horse-drawn wagons that had been used to clean up the wreckage had been left behind the military vehicles. He shuffled toward it. The horses were prancing nervously from the sound of the previous gunfire, drawing tight against the ropes that held them to a corner post. He moved behind the horses, took a handful of their droppings, and rubbed it on his clothes. A dead cat lay half hidden under a pile of the rubble, and he grabbed it by the tail.

Half a dozen soldiers worked their way through the crowd, selecting five more old men. They lined them up and forced them to their knees. Some of the women continued wailing, their voices filling the square with the sound of their desperate cries. One of them screamed and ran forward, falling upon her husband.

That was fine with Müller. Six victims now.

Behind the Germans, a cellar door to a bombed-out storefront suddenly burst open, thrown back on rusted hinges. Antoni hobbled up the stairs from the basement stairwell. Müller smiled, recognizing him instantly.

The colonel moved toward Antoni, stopping just a few feet away. Antoni stood proudly on one leg, the wooden crutch almost hidden underneath his heavy jacket. The square became very still, the crowd of villagers standing in utter silence, grateful for the sacrificial lamb.

"Antoni Geric," Müller said in a deadly voice.

Antoni looked surprised. "Sir, we've never met. And yet you know my name."

Müller sneered and placed his finger against the other man's chest. "No surprise, Mr. Geric. I know everything about you rebels. I know your faces, your families. I have made it my mission to know you very well."

"Not well enough, it seems," Antoni answered. "It took you much too long to find me. And I'm only a witless cripple. That doesn't say much about the ability of the mighty Reich."

"As you say," Müller answered grimly. "And yet here you are."

Antoni's face remained defiant. He was past anger. Past fear.

He knew exactly what was coming, and he had accepted his fate. He stared blankly, seeming to look at some unseen spot on the horizon.

"A cripple, yes you are," Müller went on. "But witless, I think not. How many bridges have you destroyed? How many trains? How many bombs have you hidden? How many of my comrades have you killed?"

"I like to think I did my part," Antoni answered tartly.

"Did your part? Yes, well, we all do our part." He glanced toward the terrified villagers. "But do you understand who else you have killed?"

Antoni remained silent. Yes, he understood.

Müller moved back toward him. "Yet in the end it doesn't matter. I found you, just like I will find the other one. And with that, my work will be done. In the meantime, look at what you've done here. Look at how many of your fellow citizens you have killed. So why don't we get this over with? Tell me where I can find Lucas Capek so that I can finish my work and go home. My men are getting anxious. All of us want to be engaged in more . . . meaningful work. The fight is coming. We don't have much time."

Antoni shifted his weight, leaning on his crutch. The colonel stared at him, waiting, then shook his head in exaggerated sadness. "You know you're going to die here, don't you, Antoni Geric?"

Antoni looked up and stared into his eyes. "It's not the first time I have thought that. But if you look at death often enough, it loses all its mystery. I hate to say it, but death and I have become friends. I know him. He knows me. I'm comfortable with him now."

"Perhaps. But if death is your friend, he has still betrayed you. He brought me to you. He brought me to these others. He will bring me to them all. So it seems, Mr. Geric, that, friendships aside, your good fortune has expired." Müller turned and motioned to the crowd again. Every eye was watching, and he smiled at their fear. Turning back to Antoni, he hissed, "Where is Lucas Capek. Tell me and I will let these people live. Defy me and a hundred of them will die here on this miserable square."

Antoni was silent, his eyes down. Müller reached out and flipped his nose. An insolent child and his father. It was the most demeaning thing he could think to do.

Antoni looked up at him and swallowed, the tendons stretching in his neck. Silence. Müller waited. "Yes, I may die here," Antoni finally whispered, "but you, sir, are already dead. Given the choice between us, I'll take my lot, I guess."

Müller seemed to shrink for a moment, then gathered himself and moved forward until his face was just inches from Antoni's. "Dying is hard work, Mr. Geric," he said. "I've seen it. It's the hardest work you will ever do." Leaning in, Müller whispered in the rebel's ear, "But I can help you. I *want* to help you. The choice is yours. I can make it easy, or I can make it slow."

Antoni pulled back and spat in the Nazi's face.

Lucas hobbled away from the crowded villagers without being noticed. He had gone nearly twenty feet when one of the German soldiers finally saw him and ran toward him with an angry stride. "Get over with the others!" he demanded with a hiss, afraid of disrupting his commander's interrogation.

Lucas kept on shuffling down the street. The Nazi took a furious step toward him and slapped his head. "Get over there!" he hissed again. He kept his voice low. The last thing he wanted was to draw attention to the fact that they had missed this man.

Lucas showed his black teeth and held out a hand as if begging.

The soldier stepped away from the filthy man. He saw the bare feet, the rotting teeth, and vacant look in his eyes. He caught a whiff of the odor and took another step back. Then he saw the dead cat in the beggar's hand and snorted in disgust. Were the colonel's execution not already under way, he would have shot him on the spot, but a gunshot at this moment would ruin the drama of his commander's scene. So he slapped him again, then kicked the filthy beggar down the street.

Passing by the first SdKfz 6, Lucas hunched over and disappeared behind it. Moving quietly, he slipped to the other side of the transport and looked back. The soldier had turned and was walking back toward the others. Lucas pulled on the rusty lever that held the tailgate in place and dropped it without a sound. The satchel was just where he expected it to be, stuffed underneath the metal bench running down the driver's side of the military transport. The emergency bag was heavy, and he had to use both hands to lift it.

Pulling it out, he felt the contents through the canvas: a medical kit, colored flares, dried food, biscuits, a map.

And a gun.

A dirty rope was thrown over a wooden streetlamp and tied to the front bumper of the nearest military transport. The other end was wrapped around Antoni's neck. They didn't take the time to tie a hangman's noose; an uneven fisherman's knot was all he got. This wasn't going to be a hanging but a suffocation, slower and far more painful, the kind of punishment the SS preferred.

"Any last words?" Müller asked him.

"I would like—"

Müller didn't let him finish. Turning away, he motioned to the driver of the military transport. The SdKfz 6 slowly backed up. The rope grew taut. Müller motioned for the driver to stop, leaving Antoni suspended from his one good leg. Antoni struggled to keep the weight off the rope, forcing himself to the very tip of his boot.

And there he stood. Everyone watched him. It would take an agonizingly long time for him to die.

Hobbling past the last of the military transports, Lucas turned and sprinted toward the alleyway that ran behind the church. Pulling the metal door back, he slipped inside, dropped the cloak, and ran for the stairs. Seconds later, he was back at the balcony window.

He looked out, his face tight with frustration and rage. Antoni was still. It was too late. There was nothing he could do!

He turned away from the window and leaned against the wall, slowly sliding to the floor. He closed his eyes, wiping away the tears that were running through the stubble on his cheeks, then hid his face in his hands. He sat without moving for a very long time, listening to the sounds of the villagers crying in the square. He looked up at the heavens and then closed his eyes again.

He didn't notice the silver locket that was lying between his feet.

Müller watched Antoni in the last of his struggles. The rebel fought to keep the weight on his one leg, but eventually his body faded and he fell limp. Müller waited, then turned around and started walking past the bodies and the patches of red snow. The villagers recoiled as he approached. He motioned to his command sergeant, then turned toward his military transport and climbed in.

Fisser shouted to his men, giving a "let's go" twirl of his finger. The Germans began to gather their men and climb into the vehicles. The villagers faded away, fear and sickness keeping them in silence.

Fisser stood to the side of the first military transport. He watched his men carefully as they loaded up the four transports. As he watched, a young German regular officer walked toward him from the center of the square. Lieutenant Acker was his name. Fisser turned as he approached. "Sir," the lieutenant said mechanically. Yes, Acker was an officer, but Fisser was SS, which meant that he was the more powerful.

The young lieutenant came to a stop beside him, then nodded to the dead men lying in the snow. "My men are regular soldiers, not *Schutzstaffel,*" he said in a low voice. "They're young. They've not yet seen combat. They haven't been exposed to . . . tactics such as this."

Fisser scowled. "Give them time," he said before he turned and walked away.

FIFTEEN

Lucas remained hidden in the church, listening to the Germans until he finally heard the sound of metal tracks tearing up the cobblestone streets as they drove away.

For a long time, he didn't move. The sun moved across the horizon, burning through the haze as the villagers took away the bodies and started scavenging again. Finally, he stood. He knew what he had to do.

He walked down the stairs, his senses tight, always listening for the sound of the German half-tracks returning. Looking toward the back of the chapel, he saw an arched door and walked toward it. It was a small bathroom, and, remarkably, fresh water still came out of the tap. He ran the ice-cold water, stripped down, and washed himself. Returning to his perch, he glanced out, checked the village square, then sat and dumped the contents of the stolen satchel on the floor: emergency rations, a small knife, maps, military flares, a Luger p08. A standard-issue weapon with eight rounds in its detachable magazine, the Luger was an effective but not an excellent gun. He lifted it, feeling the cold metal in his hands. Being caught with a weapon would mean certain death, but he no longer cared. He worked the action, then inventoried his ammunition. Thirty-two rounds. Enough to get out of trouble but not to win if it came down to a real fight.

After placing the contents back in the bag, he took the knife and walked to the balcony that looked down on the chapel. A set of heavy curtains hung down both sides of a wood carving of the Christ. "My apologies," he whispered as he tore down one of the curtains and cut two long strips. Running the lines of fabric through the metal grommets in the satchel, he fashioned a small pack. Throwing it on his back, he tested the fit. A little awkward, but it would do. He put the knife in his front pocket, stuffed the extra fabric in his pack, then moved back to the window and stared out.

His mind went back to what Melina had told him. *Go to Brzeg. It is your only hope. The train will wait for no one. Go tomorrow or it will be too late.*

Zarek stood in the shadows of an empty building that faced the square. His thin hair dripped in front of his eyes, and he shivered underneath his filthy coat. He could smell himself, tart and musky, and he sucked on a rotten tooth inside his mouth, feeling the tenderness that shot through his left jaw. He was exhausted, hungry, cold, and in a very bad mood. But the rebel had to be around here somewhere. He had not left the village. He was lurking somewhere close.

He knew the rebel wouldn't stay in one place for any longer than it took to rest and eat—at least he wouldn't if he was smart.

And the young rebel had lived through the war, which meant that he was very smart indeed.

Zarek knew the only hope he had for his granddaughter was if he could find the rebel. Short of that, he and his family were going to die. If he showed up without knowing exactly where the rebel was, this would be his last night on this earth. And as cold as he was, he knew the grave was much colder.

So he shivered and kept his eyes moving across the square.

The day passed slowly. Twice during the afternoon, the German patrols returned to round up some villagers and haul them away. As the sun set, the village grew quiet. Lucas waited until it was nearly dark, then moved carefully to the front door of the church and stepped out. Standing in the shadows, he studied the villagers carefully.

The old woman from the day before saw him from across the town square and approached him with a burlap sack in her arms. She hardly slowed as she walked by and slipped him a small pouch with two soft potatoes and three large onions. "Go," she whispered as she passed.

He touched her arm to thank her, then ducked back into the church.

Zarek's heart leapt with relief. He saw the rebel standing in the shadows of the church door. He saw the old woman walk by and hand him something as she passed. He watched the rebel turn and go back into the church.

He thought of his granddaughter and smiled.

The overcast was breaking now, leaving a large but waning moon to illuminate the low clouds with white light. The streets were nearly empty, with only a few shadows moving here and there. A group of villagers stood around their fire.

"I heard a load of turnips is coming up from Warsaw," a young mother said. "I heard that from the council. They said it was for certain."

"I heard the Americans were dropping bags of grain from airplanes," an old man offered in a mock-cheerful voice. "And the Germans are sending trainloads of oats and the Russians are sending in beef and fresh pork."

The young woman looked at him with hurt in her eyes. "It could happen," she offered. "One day things are going to have to get better. It might be this week. After all, Christmas is only a few days away. What better time to get a miracle?" A few of them nodded now in optimistic agreement, but most of the others shook their heads.

"Turkeys for Christmas!" the old man went on sarcastically. "Now, isn't that going to be a thing!"

She glared at him but didn't answer. A few minutes later, she left the fire without a word.

Zarek watched the villagers' interaction from his post near the wall, where he had stood for hours now waiting for the rebel to leave the church. Time was passing in slow motion, worse because his feet were aching from the cold. He glanced at a few black figures moving up and down the street, then returned his gaze to the dark windows of the church.

He was sure the rebel would come out any moment—but he didn't. And that didn't make any sense! Didn't he know that he had to keep moving or he would be found? Did he realize that his own people would betray him? Was he really going to sleep in the church?

Zarek was torn. He couldn't make the same mistake that he had made before. He couldn't go to Müller and lose the rebel while he was gone. He hesitated, fearful of making the wrong decision. He stared down the street behind him, then turned back to the church.

More time passed, and Zarek finally made his decision. Foolish as it was, the rebel must intend to sleep in the church. Zarek had to let Müller know. It would take him twenty minutes to get out to the SS compound. Soldiers could be here within an hour.

He turned from the church and started limping stiffly down the icy street.

Lucas stood at the balcony window a final time, looking down on the square. It was getting late enough that he doubted the Germans would return. He moved down the stairs to the chapel, stood a moment in the darkness, then walked toward the altar. Sitting on the floor beside it, he ate one of the potatoes, then shoved the rest of the food into his pack.

Standing, he walked to the front door, put his hand on the iron handle, and hesitated once again, standing motionless in the dark.

Glancing toward the east windows, he watched a series of lightning flashes in the distance from the Russian artillery attacks on the last of the fleeing German forces. Even in the church he could hear the rolling thunder. Everything was dying. He felt alone and in despair. He was leaving his fatherland, the proud kingdom of the *Poleshkva.* He knew that once he started down this road, it would be impossible to come back. Once he was on the train, there would be no getting off.

He thought a moment, then shrugged off his pack and walked back toward the altar. He pulled out his small pack of food, took out both onions and his last potato, and placed them on the altar as a final gift for the fellow countrymen he loved.

Walking to the door, he slipped outside and started walking south along the main road.

SIXTEEN

The moon was giving enough light through the scattered overcast that Lucas could see his way among the rubble. He headed west on Zervizk Street as he plotted the best route to Brzeg.

He would stick to the back roads, then cut across the unnamed forests and hills that lay to the south. From there, he would cross the Oder River and approach Brzeg from the south. It would be slow travel, with snows in the rolling hills and too much open prairie to the west that would leave him exposed. The forest would be the hardest part. Deep snows. Steep hills. Dangers in the night. But if he could make it to the forest, it would give him cover, making it much safer than traveling on the road.

But he would be walking through the middle of the chaos. There were a couple of million Russian and German soldiers all around him, the battle lines a jagged jigsaw, with Russians to the east and Germans to the west and south. He was a young man of military age in the middle of a war zone. None of them would let him pass.

He summed up his chances. He could make it to Brzeg in three days, but just barely, and only if he didn't run into trouble. Yet Melina's words kept ringing in his ears: *It is your only hope for freedom.* So although it broke his heart to think of leaving, he knew he had no choice. He would catch the last train out of Poland so that he could live. He would take the last train out of Poland so that he could be free.

Looking at the sky, he noted the moon was waning, but it was still a little more than half full. And the air was growing colder, which meant clear skies for the next couple of days.

His eyes had adjusted, and his night vision was now acute. The moon and stars seemed much brighter, and he could see dim shadows across the winter ground. The buildings were becoming more spaced out as he moved toward the outskirts of the town. Knowing there would be guards on the main roads that led into the city, he moved down a side street. Here the damage to Gorndask was acute, for he was entering the industrial area. He could see the outline of an old factory to his right, its steel girders and metal roofing peeled back like a can made of tin. The buildings to his left were mostly brick and clapboard homes that had once served the administrators of the factory. He moved to that side of the street. The snow was deeper here, the cobblestone sidewalk icy. Ahead of him, he saw a bright fire burning outside a large, square brick building. A dozen men milled around it, working by its light. He noticed the pipes going into the building and the air vents on the top. A generator building, he thought. Yes, that was what it was. They were trying to get the electricity going. He nodded at them in admiration. They would keep fighting for heat and electricity right up until the time the Russians showed up to destroy it all again.

At the end of the block was another church, this one much smaller and with a roof that was almost completely destroyed. He pushed the door back and saw half a dozen people huddled around a small fire in the corner, the smoke wafting up and out into the night through openings in the damaged roof. They were roasting a pair of rabbits over the fire, and they nodded to him as he entered but didn't invite him to join them. He lifted his chin to acknowledge them, then made his way to the other side of the chapel and lay down on one of the pews. Settling in, he listened to their quiet voices as they talked among themselves. When their meager meal was complete, they started singing Christmas hymns.

He pulled his collar around his chin and fell asleep.

SEVENTEEN

Cela glanced over her shoulder and looked at the village square. Quiet streets. A waning moon. Flashes in the distance lighting up the horizon like lightning in the thin clouds. Rumbles of artillery. Cold breath in front of their faces. Darkness all around.

She took Aron's hand and pulled him into the church, grateful for the warmer air inside the old rock chapel. He was silent, his little eyes scanning nervously around. Only a few of the candles in the window were still burning, leaving long shadows everywhere. To Cela's relief, no one was inside the chapel. Having slept in the church many nights before, the children knew where to go. Cela pulled Aron to the bathroom, and they washed their hands and faces and took a long drink. Behind the bathroom was a small storage room with a low roof and a wooden floor that smelled of lemon oil. She took a candle and they slid inside, knowing it was the warmest place in the church.

"Wait here," Cela told Aron as she turned and slipped out

of the room. She was only gone a moment before she came back. "Look at this!" she cried. She was holding a potato and two large onions in her hands. Aron's eyes grew wide, and he jumped up and ran to her. They broke the potato in half and shared it, taking bites of onion in between.

It took surprisingly little food to fill them. Cela hid the remainder inside a dirty sack and tied it protectively around her waist. They lay down together on a mattress of oily rags.

"How much longer will we stay here?" Aron asked as he closed his eyes.

Cela didn't answer for a moment. "I don't know, little brother," she finally said.

"I'm not little anymore."

"But you're always my little brother."

"I'm not little!" Aron's voice was defiant.

Cela nodded. "Of course not. You'll be a man soon."

"We can't stay here forever," Aron whispered. "We have to find our way back home."

She pulled him close and wrapped her arms around him. "Maybe this will be our home now," she answered hopefully.

His breathing was slowing down, and Cela felt his head grow heavy against her arm. "I hope not," he said, his voice a whisper. "I hope . . . we find something . . . better . . ."

He was asleep.

Cela closed her eyes as well, exhaustion and hunger making her weak.

In minutes, she was asleep.

Cela woke suddenly, her eyes flying open at the sound of the wooden door creaking on its hinges. She lifted her head to see

Melina slip into the room. She sat up, rubbing the sleep from her eyes. "Melina!" she whispered. "What are you doing here?"

"I came to tell you something."

"What is it, Melina?"

Melina nodded at Aron. "Wake him up, Cela. We have to go right now."

EIGHTEEN

That night, underneath the bombed-out ceiling of the small church, Lucas dreamt. But he didn't dream in tumbled images and painful memories of strife and war. There were no flashes of ugliness or violence or dead strangers in his arms. The dream was soft but hazily real, filled with voices of people whom he loved but had not seen in many years.

Snow fell in huge flakes that floated slowly through the air before melting on his eyebrows and the tip of his nose. It was cold, but he was warm inside a woolen jacket with a silk scarf around his neck. The city was bright with gas lanterns and electric lights in every window. He was surrounded by three-story brick and wooden buildings, and the wide streets were filled with red buses, occasional horses, and passing cars with open tops. The snow had gathered on the streets and the rooftops of the buildings, turning everything clean and white. A quartet of violinists were playing

Christmas hymns on the corner, and children were throwing snowballs at each other across the street.

He was in a hurry. He didn't want to be late. So he walked with a determined gait, his young legs taking long strides through the snow. He was breathing heavily, his breath blowing in white mist across his face as he hurried down the street. Past a bookshop. Past a small grocery with an open box of potatoes sitting underneath the portico that covered the front door. Past a large hotel, a thick Christmas tree with burning candles in the front window. Feeling a growing sense of urgency, he almost broke into a run. He stopped anxiously at the corner to let a carriage pass, glanced at the illuminated city clock on the corner, then ran across the street behind a Belvalette coupe. Reaching the other side, he slowed to catch his breath. His destination was just ahead.

The man would be waiting for him inside.

The small café was brightly lit. The wooden door was heavy, and a wave of warm, heavily scented air rushed out to meet him as he pushed it back. He shook the snowflakes off his shoulders and looked around. The man was sitting in the corner booth. Dressed in his formal military uniform, ribbons and badges and stars, he looked handsome but imposing. Lucas straightened his back, walked toward him, and slid into the booth. "Good evening, Lucas," his father greeted.

Lucas looked at him across the table. "Father," he said as he stared into his father's face. His beard was trim and tight, emphasizing the shape of his jaw, and his eyes were soft and brown. But his lips were pressed with worry.

"You know I'm leaving in the morning," his father said. It was a comment, not a question.

"Sir."

"I don't want to go—you know that, don't you, Lucas?"

Lucas nodded slowly, trying to hide his fear.

"They need me. My country needs me."

"I understand, Father."

His father leaned toward him. "There will come a time when they will need you, too."

"I hope so, Father."

"Don't hope for that, Lucas. I want you to hope for something better. Hope for a time when our nation no longer needs its young men."

Lucas started to say something, then bit his tongue and waited.

"You know that things are bad, don't you, son?"

Lucas felt his heart sink. It scared him to hear his father talk this way. "I do, sir," he answered simply.

"Evil men have brought pain and rage into this world. They have a vision of the future that is very dark indeed. But we have seen this thing before, and the world seems to find a way through it, depending on the souls of men." He stopped and stared at the hot tea on the table. "Yes, we have a choice now. But choosing isn't easy. Do you understand me, Lucas?"

"I understand, Father," Lucas answered once again.

His father turned away. "I didn't think it would turn out this way," he admitted in resignation. "I don't think that any of us did. But this is what we're left with. There is no changing it. God never promised us an easy road." His father hesitated. "But that doesn't mean He doesn't love us. You know that, don't you, Lucas?"

"I do, sir."

"You say the words. I hope you mean it."

Lucas forced a smile, then lowered his eyes, not wanting his father to see his fear. The world was crumbling all around him, every good thing in his life hanging on the edge of a cliff. His entire people, his entire nation! How could God allow this to happen?

How could any compassionate being allow so much suffering and unfairness in the world? Any god that allowed such a thing was only a god of darkness, and that was no god to him.

His father watched a deep sadness sweep across Lucas's face. Reaching across the table, he took Lucas's hand and held it so tight his knuckles turned white. "I don't know what's going to happen to us, Lucas. I can't lie to you, I don't know. But I know we can get through this. Our family can get through this. I know we can."

Lucas pressed his lips but kept his eyes down.

"Lucas, I've thought a lot about this. Many nights. Many days. And even now I don't know if I can find the right thing to say. I don't know if I—or anyone—can say something that will make a difference. But I feel compelled to try.

"You see, Lucas, sometimes I wonder too. Why would God do this? Where is the fairness? What are we supposed to learn from this great trial? It has bothered me right down the center of my soul. I have asked, and I have pleaded, and the answer has not come.

"But sometimes I think God wants to see what we will do when we don't get an answer. Sometimes God will ask us: In the absence of any evidence, what will you *choose* to believe? Which path will you follow when I don't show you the way?

"When the night is the darkest, are we still willing to fight? Will we keep on going when the only thing we have is hope?"

Lucas woke. For a dizzying moment he didn't know where he was. He saw shadows and yellow light from a dying fire. A partially open sky through a bombed-out roof. Low voices coming from the people still whispering at the front of the chapel. Then he remembered, and he closed his eyes again.

He thought back on the dream. He didn't understand it, but it left him feeling comforted. It was a good dream. It made him happy. He wanted to remember everything. So he thought back, trying to etch every detail into his mind.

The last time he had seen his father. The café back in Warsaw. The night before his father left to fight in the war. The smell of the bakery. The snow outside. The words his father said.

That was when he realized that it wasn't just a dream, it was a memory. And the memory was very real.

NINETEEN

The morning light was just beginning to shine through the broken church windows. It was clear outside, and the sun was reflecting off the new snow, creating a million points of light to illuminate the inside of the sanctuary.

Lucas woke. He lay with his eyes open, staring at the broken roof. It was chilly but not uncomfortable, and he thought back on the dream again. He could picture the old café in Warsaw. His father's uniform. The smell of baking pastries. The feel of the kitchen's heat.

The memories were coming back. They might be coming only a piece at a time, but they *were* coming, and that made him feel good.

He sat up on the pew and looked around. The refugees from the night before were gone, their fire in the corner a smoldering pit of black coals on the stone floor. He thought he was alone, but then he saw her and caught his breath.

Melina was sitting on a large wooden chair that seemed to have been set to preside over the congregation. Same white dress. Same light blue apron. Same dark hair and almond eyes.

She stood and moved toward him. Seeing what was behind her, he took another breath. On the raised platform were two sleeping children. She had covered them with a dirty blanket, and they lay side by side, their heads resting against each other.

His gut tightened up. What was she doing here?

And why the children?

He looked at the little girl's curly hair and dark skin. He remembered her from his first day in the village, standing on the pile of rubble, tense and ready to run.

"Please," the little girl had pleaded while pointing to her tummy. "Please *pan*. We are hungry."

His instincts were instantly on alert, and he shook his head while staring at Melina.

"Good morning, Lucas," she said in a quiet voice.

"Melina! What are you doing here?" he whispered.

"I brought you something."

"You brought me something?"

"Yes." She motioned toward the children. "You're going to take them with you to Brzeg."

He huffed in disbelief. "No! What are you thinking!"

"You're going to take them with you. You're going to get them on the train. You're going to save their lives."

He looked at her in angry disbelief. "You're wrong if you think I'm going to take them. You're wrong for even asking. Even if I wanted to take them, it would be impossible. It's going to be a treacherous journey just to make it on my own. I don't have time to carry two little children." He was struggling to keep his voice low so the children wouldn't wake. "And think about this, Melina. Traveling with me is *guaranteed* to get them killed. You know who

I am! You know who is out there hunting me down. Do you think the SS colonel cares a whit if they are children? How many Polish children has he already killed?"

She looked at him, a calm expression on her face. "If you don't take them, they will die here. You know that as well as I do. The Russians are just a few days away. Once they get here, things will only get worse." She paused and smiled at him knowingly. "No more potatoes. No more onions."

Lucas didn't seem to notice.

"If you don't help them, these two angels are going to starve to death," she started pleading.

"So will ten thousand others! It's just the cost of war."

She looked at him a moment, a shadow of doubt passing over her face. It was the first time that he had seen it, and it caused a pang of sadness and regret. He lowered his voice and moved toward her. "I'm sorry. I really am. But traveling with me would be a death sentence."

"Lucas, if you don't help them, they will die. They don't deserve that. None of these children do. Look at them, Lucas. Look into their faces. You are their only hope."

"If I take them, I will kill them!" He jabbed an angry finger to the east. "*He* will kill them. It is hopeless. So much is hopeless . . ."

"This isn't about having hope or being hopeless. This is about the lives of these two children."

Lucas shook his head in frustration. "You don't have any right to—"

"What do you do when there's no hope, Lucas?" Melina interrupted.

Lucas froze. He stared at her, his mouth open. "What did you say?" he muttered.

"What are you willing to do, Lucas?" She took a step toward him. "When the night is the darkest, what are you willing to do?"

Lucas stared at her, unable to speak. He slowly shook his head, his mind flashing back.

When the night is the darkest, are we still willing to fight? Will we keep on going when the only thing we have is hope?

He shook his head again and stared at her.

How did she know!

Melina reached out to touch him, stopping just short of his hand. "Even if we don't know the way—and neither of us does—you have to ask yourself, are you still willing to fight?" She stepped aside so that he could see the children. "I can't make you do this, Lucas. The choice is always yours. But if you're willing to take on a last battle, surely this one is worth the fight."

TWENTY

Colonel Müller sat in the library in an old leather chair, an untouched tray of sausage and potatoes sitting on the table beside him. His tan combat fatigues hung loosely on his frame, and his pant leggings were tucked into his black leather boots. His dark hair, normally slicked back, hung in strands at the side of his head, and his eyes were red and bleary. He had adjusted his holster so that he could sit more comfortably; his left hand rested upon the butt of the dark pistol at his hip. He pulled a last drag on an unfiltered cigarette, then threw the soggy butt on the wooden floor between his feet. The number of discarded cigarettes around him indicated he had not moved from the chair since at least the night before. But morning sunlight now slanted through the wooden-framed window and cast his face in glaring white light.

Soldiers walked up and down the hallway outside the double doors, their anxious voices adding urgency to the air. There wasn't panic, but it was close, with the sound of violent artillery thunder constantly in the air. With every rumble, the windows shuddered from the percussion of the Russian fire. No one spoke to Müller, leaving him alone in his chair.

Another roll of thunder vibrated the picture window that looked upon the east lawn, and the *Schutzstaffel* officer couldn't help but turn toward the sound. The rumble was so powerful he thought it might shake the glass right out of its frame. The Russians were very close. His dark eyes glinted with cold emotion and he cursed violently.

His command sergeant stood at attention five feet to his right, waiting for his commander to speak. Sergeant Fisser held his metal helmet underneath his arm, and a rifle was strapped across his back. He had been waiting for more than ten minutes. He wearily shifted his weight from one foot to the other. The room was uncomfortably hot from a large fire blazing in the fireplace, and he quickly wiped the sweat from his brow.

"Fire is a curious thing," Müller said.

Fisser didn't answer.

"Yes, it brings warmth on winter days, but it has a dark side as well."

Fisser turned his eyes toward the sizzling fire.

"What a horrible way to die," Müller concluded.

"It is, sir. And I'm sorry."

Müller took a drag. "Which squad lost the emergency bag?" he asked. He kept his eyes straight ahead as he talked.

"Fouling squad, sir."

"And when was the equipment taken?"

"We think that it was yesterday, sir. It was discovered when the squad inventoried their equipment and ammunition."

"Losing a weapon upon the battlefield is a serious offense, isn't it, Command Sergeant?"

The sergeant clicked his heels. "I am certain that the men are aware of the penalties, sir."

"So the rebel has a weapon?"

"It is a possibility, sir."

"It is not a mere possibility, Command Sergeant, it is a fact. So now I have to ask myself, how many of my men are going to die because we couldn't secure our own weapons?"

Fisser clicked his heels again.

"Identify the man who is responsible for this failure," Müller said. "See that he is punished. I leave it up to you to determine the method, but you will report your decision back to me."

The sergeant's expression became incredulous and his lips grew tight. He glanced toward the booming sound outside the window, then turned back to his commander and swallowed hard. A long moment of silence passed. "Permission to speak freely, sir?" he finally asked.

The colonel reached down, lifted a china cup, and touched the hot liquid to his lips. After placing the cup back on the table, he answered dryly, "Permission granted."

"Colonel Müller, forgive me, but I don't think a single weapon is the greatest of our concerns."

Müller picked up the cup and sipped at it again. Fisser moved his helmet from one hand to the other. "Sir, again, if I could?"

Müller lifted a dismissive hand to silence him, held it for a long moment, then dropped it to his lap and nodded his consent.

"Sir, we have been given orders to retreat."

Müller almost hissed. "The German army *does not retreat!*"

Fisser quickly caught himself. "Of course not, sir. I apologize. We have been ordered to reassemble."

"The German army does not retreat!" Müller hissed again. He paused, breathing deeply. A moment of silence passed. "And remember, there is the operation against the Allies in the Ardennes. Half a million of our brothers fight there. It may prove to be the battle that turns the tide. But if not, we will reassemble and continue the fight."

Fisser hesitated, then shook his head, seeming to make a fateful decision. "Sir, the German army has been reassembling for about a thousand miles now. We have to prepare to defend the Fatherland. That's the only thing that matters now."

Müller jumped instantly to his feet, china crashing to the floor. He moved with surprising speed toward the sergeant, stopping only inches from his face. "It is *not* the only thing that matters!"

Fisser took a few steps back. Müller glared at him in rage. A long moment passed. Müller finally turned back to his chair, kicked away the broken china, and sat down, staring back into the fire.

Fisser took a careful step toward him. "Sir." His voice was soft and submissive. "We cannot face the Russians. Not with the few men we have. If we delay here another day, every one of us will die here."

"We stay. We still have rebel forces in the area."

"We have a single member of the resistance," Fisser argued. "That is not a rebel force, sir."

"I will not betray the Fatherland. I will not betray my *Führer.*"

The sergeant stared at him, dumbfounded. The thought of being captured by the Russians had suddenly given him a great deal of nerve. "Sir, you cannot ignore the general's orders."

"I don't care who gave us orders. We will not reassemble until our mission is complete."

A moment of silence followed. "Sir, you know what the Bolsheviks do to captured SS officers: the torture, the insides pulled out. Would you do that to your men?"

Müller lit another cigarette, then turned to glare at Fisser. "We will face that when it happens. And if it does, you will not save one bullet for yourself. You will fight them till your magazine is empty, and then you will stand and take the consequences like a man."

The sergeant closed his eyes. He knew it was decided, even if it meant the death of them all. He kept his head down for a moment, a look of resignation on his face. The room was quiet except for the occasional pops from the fire and the deep-throated rumbles against the window.

Hearing something new, the sergeant glanced toward the east. Occasional bursts of short thunder were now mixed among the deep artillery fire. The colonel turned toward the window, following the sergeant's eyes.

"German tanks firing to cover our . . . *reassembly,*" the sergeant said.

The colonel listened a moment, then threw his cigarette on the floor. He waved a hand toward the village. "I'm supposed to believe a Devil stood among them and no one even noticed?"

"We searched the area. We talked to everyone we could find. No one remembered seeing him."

"Of course they saw him. Of course they knew he was a rebel. And someone knows where he went."

"Sir, we could bring some of them in for questioning."

"What does it matter now?" Müller snapped. "Any information would be hours old." He stood and moved to a map that had been pinned to the wood-paneled wall and stared at it angrily, then glanced toward the door. "Fool of a beggar," he sneered. "Bring him in."

The sergeant moved quickly to the door and pulled it back. The old man was waiting, sheer terror in his eyes. The sergeant pulled him into the room and Zarek fell forward, landing on his knees. He didn't try to stand. He didn't talk. He kept his head down, awaiting his execution. The SS colonel stepped to him and pulled his head back to look into his eyes. "I asked you to do one simple thing, and you have failed me. Now what am I to do with you, my friend?"

"Sir, I swear he was in the church."

"But he is gone. And I have nothing."

Zarek looked like he might throw up on the floor. "I thought he was going to stay the night there," he sobbed, dirty tears sliding down his cheeks. "I had to come and tell you that I had found the rebel."

"But we don't have the rebel. We don't have him because he wasn't where you promised he would be."

The man sobbed again and the SS officer grabbed him by the coat, lifted him up, and threw him against the wall. The old man pressed his face against the dark paneling as if he were trying to melt into the wood. The colonel pulled him back and jabbed a finger at the map. "Look at this!" he sneered. "You know your people. You know how they think. You know this area. Now look at this map and tell me where he would go!"

The beggar stared with wide eyes. His mind raced, his heart thumping wildly in his chest. He braced himself against the wall as he studied the military map, then lifted a trembling hand and touched it, moving his fingers east toward the Russians and then west toward the fleeing German army. He briefly moved his hand north, and then he hesitated.

He remembered something he had heard a couple of nights before. A rumor. Whispers in the shadows. Impossible to believe. But he was going to die if he didn't come up with something and it was the only thing he had.

"I hear rumors," he said.

"Of course you do, my little spy."

"There is supposed to be a train," he stammered quickly. "A refugee train on Christmas morning."

"And where could we find this train on Christmas morning?"

"Brzeg," the old man said.

TWENTY-ONE

Lucas stopped and looked around. Aron was on his shoulders, and Lucas kept his hands on the boy's legs to hold him in place. Cela walked up behind him, following in his tracks. The snow was six inches deep, and her little legs struggled to keep up. "Why did you stop?" she huffed as she came to rest beside him.

Lucas glanced down at her. "I just wanted to look around."

"You don't have to stop for me," she shot back. "I can keep up."

Lucas wiped a bead of cold sweat off his brow, then looked down at her again. "I wasn't stopping for you. I just want to make sure I know where we're going." He stomped his feet in the snow and took a look around. The forest was thick with high pines and low maples. The rolling terrain descended to his right. Beyond the tree line, he knew the hills dropped down to flat terrain. Villages there. Farms. Retreating Germans along the narrow roads. In front of him, beyond the forest, was the Oder River. Beyond that, Brzeg.

After two days of walking, they were almost there.

Lucas pointed to a clearing under the trees. "Let's take a rest."

"You don't need to rest for me," Cela answered tartly. Lucas couldn't help but smile.

"I want to get down," Aron said, kicking off of Lucas's shoulders and dropping into the snow. He ran to the clearing. Lucas and Cela followed.

The trees broke in front of them, the terrain dropping steeply toward the flat. Lucas studied the valley before him. Two black ribbons ran through the snow-dirt roads. He observed occasional columns of soldiers walking west, with military vehicles here and there, the tail end of the humiliating German defeat. On the other side of the trees, he could hear explosions as the Russians chased them toward the German border. He turned to face the children, then nodded to the bare ground under the nearest tree and sat down. Cela sat beside him, and he shook off his pack and started pulling out what remained of their rations. Behind the tree, a white rabbit appeared, moving cautiously toward them.

Aron saw the rabbit. "Shhh . . ." he whispered as he slowly started inching toward it. The rabbit backed away but didn't run. Aron moved so slowly it was almost impossible to detect. He crouched, his hands extended, ready to snatch the rabbit. Lucas smiled, knowing it was hopeless. "Get him, Aron," he whispered.

Cela watched her brother and whispered to Lucas, "I've seen him do it before."

Lucas glanced at her, not believing.

"No, he can," Cela said. Her voice was barely audible. "I don't know how he does it. It's like magic. But he's fed us more than once."

Lucas seemed impressed, his eyes opening wide in admiration. Whether he was sincere or not, Cela couldn't tell. Aron took another step through the snow. The rabbit ran. Aron continued stalking. The rabbit came to a stop twenty feet away. Aron stalked. Lucas watched him, then glanced awkwardly to the little girl beside him.

"Cela, right?" he asked.

Cela looked disgusted. "You don't know my name yet?" she scolded.

"No, I do. I'm just . . . you know, making sure. So, Cela. That's a pretty name."

"Cela Danielle," she added while staring at the food Lucas had shaken out of his pack and spread across a patch of bare ground. They had made the rations last, but barely, and the food was nearly gone.

Lucas watched her hesitate, then reached down and took one of the remaining crackers. He peeled away the brown wrapper and considered it. Dark brown. Thick. Grain pulp and flour paste. He took a large bite. It tasted like glue and paper. But he didn't care. He was famished. All of them were.

Cela watched him, then reached down and took a cracker too, unwrapped it quickly, and put it to her lips.

"How old are you, Cela Danielle?" Lucas asked.

"How old do you think I am?" she challenged as she took a small bite.

"Please don't make me do this."

Cela was smiling now. "How old do you think?"

Lucas hesitated. He didn't like the game. "I don't know. Somewhere between five and fifteen. I'm not good at this kind of thing."

"I'll give you a hint. I'm older than five."

"I could have got that much, Cela."

She smiled at him, then took another nibble at her cracker.

Lucas glanced over his shoulder to check on Aron. The chase with the rabbit went on. "All right," he said. "I'll guess eleven."

Cela suddenly looked very proud. "You really mean that?"

"Sure, why not."

Cela started laughing. "Because you're wrong! I'm eight. But I'll be nine next month."

Lucas looked surprised. "Eight? Really? That seems so young."

"I don't feel young," she said. Her voice was suddenly very serious. She took another tiny bite of her cracker but kept her eyes focused on the ground.

"You've done a good job taking care of Aron," Lucas said.

"He's my brother."

Lucas watched her nibble. "You don't have to do that, Cela. You don't have to be so careful. We have enough to eat."

Cela shook her head. "There's never enough to eat."

"There is now. We've made good progress. We should make it to the Oder River by tonight. Brzeg is just on the other side." Lucas hesitated as he thought. "Of course, we have to figure out how to get across the lowland and the roads without being seen. And how to cross the river. That could be a bit of a problem." He turned and smiled at her. "But we'll figure it out."

Both of them turned to watch Aron sneaking up on the rabbit. He moved slowly through the snow, then gave sudden chase. The rabbit easily hopped away and stopped. It was almost as if they were playing a game. Aron started sneaking up on it again.

Cela absently fingered a silver locket around her neck. Lucas turned to her and saw it. He leaned over and touched it with his finger. "That's very pretty."

Cela pulled away. "I found it," she said defensively. "In the church. I didn't take it."

"I know you didn't, Cela. In fact, I think I might know who it belonged to."

Cela looked disappointed as she reached up and started to unlock the chain.

"No, Cela. You keep it. I'm sure she would want you to have it anyway."

Cela smiled at him weakly. They ate in silence until Cela finished her cracker. She reached out toward a can of meat, looked at Lucas as if waiting for his disapproval, then took the can, opened it, and started eating hungrily. Lucas watched. She ate as if she were starving, which of course she was. Cela turned to him, her mouth crammed with food. "You seem kind of sad," she said.

Lucas smiled at her. "I'm not sad. I'm just careful. I want to make sure we get there safely."

"No. I think you're sad." When he didn't answer, she took the lid of her canned meat and licked it clean, then ran her finger around the inside of the can and licked it as well. She wiped her lips, then glanced at Lucas, embarrassed.

"The meat is pretty good," he said.

She nodded eagerly and leaned back against a tree. "Tomorrow is Christmas," she said.

"Yes. I guess we're catching a Christmas train out of Poland."

Cela studied him. "Can I ask you something?"

"Sure."

"Do you believe in Christmas?"

Lucas's brow furrowed without him knowing it. "I'm not sure what you mean?"

"Do you believe in . . . you know . . . Christmas?"

"I don't know, Cela Danielle," he answered carefully. "That's kind of like asking if I believe in September. Sure, I believe in Christmas. I know it's coming. Tomorrow will be Christmas Day."

"That's not what I meant. But you knew that. What I meant is, do you believe in, you know, all of the things about Christmas Day?"

Lucas shrugged. "Sure. Why not?"

"What you really mean is no."

"No, Cela, that's not what I meant."

She smiled at him sadly, as if they had just shared an unhappy secret. "It's okay," she said. "Sometimes I don't believe it either."

Lucas leaned toward her, staring into her eyes. "You're too young to think that way."

"If you had seen the things that I've seen, you might not say that."

They fell silent, both of them thinking. Lucas picked up a stick and examined it nervously, then took the knife and started sharpening one end. Cela watched him a moment. "I trust you," she said. "If you're saying . . ."

"I'm not saying anything, Cela."

"So you think I should believe?"

"I don't know. I guess so. Most people do."

She squared her shoulders as if she had just made an important decision. "Okay then. For now, we'll both believe in Christmas."

Lucas jabbed the stick into the ground. "Tell me about your family."

Cela motioned toward her little brother. "That's my family."

"What about your mom and dad?"

Cela shrugged. "I don't know."

"You don't know? What do you mean?"

"We stopped getting letters," she answered simply, as if that explained everything.

Lucas waited. "I'm not sure what you mean," he finally said.

Cela took a deep breath, her eyes seeming to focus on nothing.

"My dad was in the army. He wrote us every chance he could. But then we just stopped getting letters. That was it. No explanation. No word from the war ministry. Nothing. It was like he just disappeared. Then when the Germans came, they sent all of us young ones out to the country. We didn't have any choice, they just sent us away. Every day our mother would write us. Every single day. But then . . . her letters just stopped coming too."

"I'm very sorry," Lucas answered.

"Lots of people are sorry about a lot of things."

Lucas stared ahead, then jabbed the stick into the snow again. "There's no one else in your family?"

Cela took a breath and seemed to hold it, then let it out with a sigh. "I had an older brother and sister, but I really don't remember them. My sister died of pneumonia right after the Germans invaded. I never really knew her. My only memory of my brother was one year he was supposed to come home for Christmas. I was so excited. I remember waiting on Christmas Eve, staring out the window. But he never came."

Lucas watched her a moment, then took his pack and started to gather their gear, packing up the few remnants of food. "We need to go," he said.

Cela didn't move. "We're just trying to get home," she said.

Lucas kept on working. "That's all any of us are trying to do."

Cela reached out for his hand. "But we're going to be okay now, right? You're going to take us to the train? We'll be safe there. Someone will be able to help me take care of my little brother. You're going to help us, right?"

Lucas touched her gently on the head. "Yes, Cela. That's what I'm going to do."

TWENTY-TWO

Müller stood on the shabby porch of the old farmhouse. "Come on, let's move!" he commanded his men. They scrambled urgently around him, loading gear and ammunition, checking weapons, taking the last of their supplies from the farmhouse and brick barn they had occupied for the night. Knowing they were the last of the German army within at least twenty miles, all of them were nervous. The Russian advance squads were so close the German soldiers could almost smell the fire from their artillery, but only a few of them realized that the war had almost leapfrogged over them, much of the rocket fire passing over their heads.

Four German SdKfz 6 half-track transports were lined up on the dirt road that led to the farmhouse. Forty soldiers were busy getting ready to move out. A few of them, the leaders, were SS officers, but the others were regular army soldiers: younger, softer, less determined, less violent, far less battle hardened.

Zarek cowered at the side of the broken porch, trying as hard as he could to appear invisible to the German soldiers. He kept his head down, his eyes avoiding their suspicious stares as he waited like an obedient dog for his master to call his name. Every moment, he thought of his hut, his warm wood stove, his blind daughter, and the angel he called *dzeiko.*

If I cast my soul to hell for what I've done, then I go there with a heart as good as any man's, he thought.

Müller leaned against one of the pillars holding up the slanted roof and smoked as he watched his men work. His black leather coat reached down to the top of his boots, and he held black leather gloves in one hand. The death skull on his officer's cap and silver colonel rank were the only patches of silver on his uniform. He called out again, yelling at his men, "Let's go! Move! Move!"

Sergeant Fisser approached him from behind, walking through the old wooden door that had protected the entrance to the farmhouse for more than a hundred years. Seeing Fisser, the other soldiers stopped their work and looked at him, their faces expectant. Hopeful. More than a hint of frustration showed in their expressions. They knew they were on a suicide mission. The sergeant was their only hope.

A young German lieutenant worked among his soldiers, hoisting metal boxes of ammunition into the back of the lead vehicle. He wore lieutenant rank, but he looked older than most, with light skin and determined eyes. When the war had started, he was barely out of high school; now he'd seen enough blood and anguish to fill a lifetime. He stopped and stole a glance at Fisser as the SS sergeant walked across the porch. Fisser looked at him and shook his head. Lieutenant Acker frowned and quickly looked away.

Hearing Fisser's footsteps, Müller scowled. The command sergeant came to a stop directly behind him. Müller didn't turn around.

"Sir, General Werner is on the line," Fisser announced as quietly as he could. He didn't want the other men to hear. It would only invite more fear and discouragement if they knew.

Müller ignored him while motioning to his men. "Keep it moving!" he shouted. "We've got a mission to complete!"

The soldiers turned and got back to their work.

"Sir, General Werner . . ." Fisser said again.

"I heard you," Müller answered coldly.

Fisser took another step toward him, but Müller lifted a hand to stop him. "Sergeant Fisser, what do you expect General Werner is going to tell me?"

"Sir, I suppose he's going to repeat his instructions from last night."

"I suspect that is correct. Now, I don't suppose the tactical situation has either changed or improved. It would seem, then, that the general and I are having a disagreement on our combat priorities."

"Sir . . ."

"Mount up! Let's go!" Müller shouted to his men.

The soldiers reluctantly started climbing into the open backs of the gangly transports.

Müller glared at them, then finally turned to Fisser. He took an angry step toward him and lowered his voice. "Let me ask you something," he hissed. "Do you think for one moment that I would hesitate to expend my life in defense of the Fatherland?"

"Sir, I know you would not."

"Indeed, I would not. My commitment is not in doubt. So let me be clear. If you ever challenge me again, I'll string you up and light you on fire. Do you understand me, Command Sergeant?"

Fisser stared straight ahead. "Yes, sir, I do."

Five minutes later, the loaded German SdKfz 6 half-tracks tracked down the muddy farm lane that connected with the main road. Müller stood in the open cabin of the lead transport, and the small convoy came to a stop. Just beyond the farm lane, the road split. Müller hesitated, then pushed the metal door back, stepped out of the half-track, and walked across the frozen mud, stopping at the fork in the road. Fisser got out of the second vehicle and walked to his side, a folded map in hand. Zarek walked behind him, blowing into his clenched fists.

Müller studied what lay before him. A thick forest. Rising terrain. One of the roads led toward the forest, then turned abruptly to avoid the high ground and heavy trees. A narrow dirt road split off, winding up the side of the gentle hill. To his right, far in the distance, he could see the outlines of a small village, the black steeple of a rock church rising above the cluster of houses. An ancient rock fence surrounded the unnamed village. Beyond that, so far in the distance that it was barely visible, he could see a silver ribbon run down from the north. The nearly frozen Oder River glinted in the sun. Müller pointed beyond the river. "It's more than eleven miles to Brzeg."

Fisser unfolded his map and studied it. "Yes, sir. Seventeen, to be exact."

Müller thought as he stared at the forest. "He won't follow the road. He'll cut across the high ground, staying in the cover of the trees."

Fisser nodded agreement. "What do you make of the reports that he's with two children?"

Müller glanced back at Zarek. "What say you, my little Polish friend?"

Zarek took a step forward. "He has no family here," he said with exaggerated confidence. "Why would he be traveling with children? It seems unlikely. Perhaps impossible. What would any children be to him?"

Müller studied him suspiciously. The look on his face made it clear that he took everything Zarek said with great suspicion.

"It does seem unlikely, sir," Fisser interjected. "Where would these children come from? Why would he take the risk? They would only slow him down. And look at those hills. The snow is blown and very deep in places. If he is traveling now with children, all he has done is put them in great danger."

Müller turned back to stare at the rising terrain before him. "If he's alone, he's going to stay to the forest. If not, if he really is traveling with a couple of Polish child-rats, he'll have to stay to lower ground. It is not possible he would take a pair of children through the uplands and the forest. He'd stay low, toward the village." Müller sounded confident.

"Should we call back the patrols we sent along the forest road, then?" Fisser asked.

Müller glanced down at his watch. "What time did we send them out?"

"Daybreak, sir. Two vehicles. Fifteen men."

Müller thought, then shook his head. "No. Keep Schmitz and Zindal on the forest road. We can handle the main roads with the men we have here. I want patrols on every trail. If we haven't found him by nightfall, we'll pull back and regroup. The Devil can't cross the river without freezing. The water would be the death of him. If that were to happen, I'd feel cheated. But he's not that stupid. He's going to—he's got to—make it to one of the bridges. That is where we'll get him. If we don't find him by dusk, we'll concentrate on the bridges that lead to Brzeg."

TWENTY-THREE

The pines started to sway as the sun rose to the midpoint in the sky, creating a stir of wind from the heat that bounced off the dark hills. Lucas collected all their gear and stood, hoisting the makeshift pack onto his back. "We need to keep moving," he said. "I don't want to get caught out when it gets dark."

Cela stood up and turned in the direction they had been walking. "Will we be there by tomorrow morning?"

"If nothing goes wrong."

Cela sighed. "Something always goes wrong."

Lucas hesitated, then nodded. "It seems that way, doesn't it? But we're going to make it. If we can just get to . . ."

The sound of braying dogs tracking their prey suddenly arose from the other side of the rising terrain. Angry. Vicious. Dogs on a hungry trail. Both of them looked to where the sound was coming from, Cela ducking suddenly to Lucas's side. "Where is Aron?" she cried.

Lucas turned and looked around in fear.

Aron was gone.

Cela started running. "Aron! Aron!" she screamed. Her voice was thick with fear.

Lucas hesitated, looking toward the hill where Aron had been chasing the snowy rabbit. He saw the little boy's tracks in the fresh snow. They headed toward the top of the hill. There, the trees were thicker, the snow deeper, having been blown into drifts. Aron's tracks disappeared over the crest of the hill.

Toward the sound of the braying dogs.

Lucas took off running through the snow. He passed Cela in just a few strides, following Aron's tracks toward the top of the hill. Cela struggled along desperately behind him. The sound of the dogs got closer. It was a terrifying sound. Cela was crying now, tears streaming down her face as she ran. "Aron! Aron! Where are you!"

Lucas glanced back and slowed, extending a hand to help her. She looked up and cried out to him, "Go! Go! Please go and find him!"

Lucas hesitated, then turned and ran, leaving Cela behind. Sixty seconds later, he came to the crest of the hill. Slowing, he reached under his coat, pulled out the handgun, cocked it, and held it near his thigh. Crouching now, he inched toward the top of the hill.

Then he heard something that made his blood chill, and he dropped even lower toward the ground. A deep rumble. To his right. Coming from the dirt road that was on the other side of the trees. His brow furrowed and he stopped, trying to catch his breath so he could listen. He stared at the trees to his right. From where he stood he could see they dropped away, falling toward the bottom of the hill. He heard the sound of engines grinding to a stop, then silence, then the sound of slamming doors.

Lucas glanced ahead, looking desperately at Aron's tracks in the snow, then turned and sprinted toward the trees. Falling into the snow beneath them, he inched forward, then lifted a hand and pushed a pine branch aside. Two hundred yards below, he saw the muddy road and a German SdKfz 6 half-track. A dozen German soldiers milled around the vehicle. Two of the soldiers were standing near the front bumper. A map was spread across the hood between them. They were close enough that he could hear their voices but far enough away that he couldn't understand what they said. He slowly backed up, pushing through the snow. Climbing out from underneath the trees, he turned and ran back toward Aron's footprints in the snow.

The dogs had stopped howling. And Cela was nowhere to be found.

He stared down at his weapon, glanced back toward the soldiers, then stuffed the gun back into his pocket and started moving the last thirty steps up to the top of the hill.

As he crested the hill, the terrain flattened out. He saw a fallen tree. Aron was kneeling in the snow beside it. The white rabbit was caught in a wire snare, and Aron was trying desperately to free it. He had his hands around the rabbit and was pulling at the snare. Three angry dogs circled him, confused and barely held at bay. The dogs had fallen silent, though they occasionally moved forward to growl at their prey. Behind the log, an old farmer was running forward, a menacing club in his hand. He whistled to his dogs, and they pulled back. He hadn't seen Aron yet, for he was hidden behind the log. Running forward, he finally saw him.

"What are you doing, boy!" His snarl was as angry as his dogs.

Aron ignored him, focusing on extracting the rabbit.

"What are you doing, boy!" the farmer hissed again. "Leave my dinner be!" Aron kept working at the wire snare, and the farmer lunged forward, grabbed him by the hair, and threw him back into the snow. The dogs resumed their frenzied barking, and the farmer shouted and gestured. They ran off into the trees in the direction they had come from.

Aron looked up at the farmer defiantly. "It's my rabbit," he said.

The farmer took a step toward him and studied the child. "Who are you, boy?" he demanded.

Aron started crawling through the snow, pushing around the farmer's knees toward the rabbit. The old man kicked him back, then pinned him down with his right foot. "What are you doing out here all alone?" He suddenly caught himself and straightened up to look around. "Are you by yourself?" he wondered out loud.

He heard the crunch of snow and turned to see Lucas walking toward him. The farmer instinctively moved his club to his right hand and lifted it. "Who are you?" he demanded.

Lucas placed his hands before him, signaling submission. "We're just passing through. We mean no trouble. We'll be on our way." He took a couple of steps forward, and the farmer reached under his coat and pulled out a hunting knife. The blade was rusty-red with dried animal blood, eight inches long and serrated on the top. Lucas stared at it a moment, then looked at the farmer once again.

"Stand your ground!" the farmer commanded.

Lucas stopped and lifted both of his hands again. He heard the far-off sound of voices drifting through the trees, and he glanced back toward the German soldiers. If the farmer heard the sound, he didn't show it, keeping all of his attention on the two intruders on his land.

"There's no reason for someone like you to be here," the farmer said. Keeping his eyes on Lucas, he reached down and lifted Aron by the coat and pulled him close. "A dozen soldiers passed through my place just a bit ago. They were looking for someone. I wonder who that was?"

Lucas glanced again toward the sound of the German soldiers, then extended his hands. "Just give me the boy and we'll be on our way," he said in a quiet voice.

"I wonder if the Germans would want to know about two strangers on my land?" the farmer said suspiciously.

Lucas took two more steps toward him. "Give me the boy," he said again.

The farmer cocked his head. "Why aren't you in the army? You should be off with all the others." He pulled Aron tight against his leg.

"Just give me the boy."

The farmer bent, grabbed Aron's head, and locked his arm around it.

"Aron, come here!" Lucas hissed.

Aron started to whimper in pain and fear. The farmer slapped him. Lucas moved his right hand toward his jacket pocket where he had hidden his gun. "Aron, come to me!" he commanded.

The farmer picked Aron up and held him off the ground, holding the knife menacingly close to the boy's throat. Lucas took another step toward him.

Five more steps to go.

"Stay back or I will kill him!" the farmer shouted.

A high-pitched scream suddenly sounded from the farmer's right.

The farmer turned to see a little girl running toward him from the grove of trees, a large stick in her hand. "Aron!" Cela cried as she ran toward them. Confused, the farmer took a step toward her. Lucas rushed forward, grabbed the farmer by the coat, and spun him around. Aron fell into the snow and covered his head, then crawled out of the way. The farmer lifted the knife and swung it violently. Lucas dodged it expertly. The farmer cursed and swung again. Lucas easily stepped back. Now the farmer's face showed real fear. He backed away, measuring the stranger, then lunged again. Lucas waited until he was extended, then struck, hitting the farmer in the face, almost knocking him down. The farmer touched his bleeding eye, cursed violently, and swung again. Lucas stepped easily aside, then hit the man again. The farmer continued to curse in rage as he lunged and swung at Lucas's head. Lucas delivered a final blow, and the farmer fell into the snow and didn't move.

Cela ran to Aron and folded him into her arms. Both of them were sobbing. Lucas dropped beside them and pulled them both close. "Shhh . . ." he whispered quietly. "Shhh . . . it's going to be all right."

Ten minutes later they were walking through the snow, following their tracks back the way they had come. Lucas was holding Aron in his arms, and Cela walked beside them. Aron clutched the dead rabbit by its legs.

Lucas looked at Cela, then reached down to help her through the snow. "That was pretty good, coming at him from behind like that," he said.

Cela looked up proudly. "I thought you might need a little diversion."

"Very clever," Lucas said.

Cela glanced back toward the top of the hill where they had left the farmer. "He's going to go and tell the Germans."

"Yes. He probably will."

Cela's face was suddenly drawn and tight. "You should have . . ." She hesitated.

Lucas looked at her and shook his head. "We'll be okay."

"I've thought that before. It turned out I was wrong. If he goes back and tells the others. . . ." She looked at Aron, who was listening to her carefully. "You know what you should have done," she said.

"We'll have time to put distance between us."

They kept on walking until Aron pulled away from Lucas and said, "I got the rabbit."

Lucas nodded at him proudly. "Yes, you did."

"I wasn't going to let that other man take it from me. It was my rabbit. I had it first."

"Yes, Aron, you did."

"It's Christmas Eve. I want to cook my rabbit for Christmas dinner."

Lucas looked at him and smiled. "We'll do that, Aron. We'll have a Christmas dinner later on tonight."

They walked a few minutes in silence, and then Cela reached up and took Lucas by the hand.

TWENTY-FOUR

The sky was growing dark, the sun dipping toward the low hills and causing the shadows from the trees to stretch over the snow like ink stains across the landscape. Flashes of light illuminated the horizon, but there was now lightning in the north as well. Patches of clouds were moving in, and the white winter moon would soon break above the eastern horizon. German *Messerschmitt* fighters were flying overhead, their engines angrily buzzing above the clouds. Russian *Yaks* sounded as well, though they were smaller and not as loud.

Lucas kept the fire just hot enough to cook the rabbit he had stretched on a stick above the flames. Aron kept his hands extended toward the heat while eyeing the rabbit hungrily. Drops of grease sometimes fell, kicking up slivers of yellow flame.

The wood was wet, and Lucas had a hard time controlling the smoke. He'd placed a couple of pine branches over the flames to help disperse it, but he continued to look at it worriedly as it climbed into the sky.

"When can we eat it?" Aron asked as Lucas turned the rabbit just a bit.

"Soon," Lucas answered.

Cela sat down and smiled as she watched the cooking meat. "It's going to be a glorious Christmas dinner," she said.

Four miles to the east, Müller stood on a narrow road on the edge of the thick forest. The Oder River was just before him, and the setting sun illuminated chunks of ice that floated with the current. Zarek stood behind him. Fisser remained by the side of his vehicle, surrounded by half a dozen German regulars. All of them were waiting for Müller to make a decision.

The colonel looked down at his map, then folded it up and tucked it in his pocket. He pulled out another cigarette, and Zarek quickly stepped forward to light it. Müller nodded toward the forest. "If he's not out there, then you and I are going to have a hard conversation," he said to Zarek.

Zarek nodded anxiously but didn't reply.

Müller took a long drag, his eyes always on the forest. "He's not along the road." Another drag. Another smoky breath. "He's up there in the forest." Another drag. "He has to be there somewhere."

The colonel moved his head from north to south, then stopped and leaned forward. Reaching behind him without turning around, he motioned to the sergeant. "Field glasses."

Fisser moved quickly to his vehicle and returned with a set of binoculars. Müller lifted them to his eyes, focused, then dropped them and pointed for the others. "Can you see that?"

Fisser concentrated on the spot where his commander was pointing, squinting his eyes.

"Smoke," Müller said.

Fisser nodded. "I see it now, sir."

"That's got to be him," Müller said with confidence.

"You would think so, Colonel," Zarek jumped in. Müller lifted his field glasses again while Fisser scowled at Zarek. The last thing he needed was for the old man to give the colonel encouragement in this insanity.

"It could be the rebel," Fisser said carefully. "But, sir, it could be something else."

Müller huffed. "Such as?" he asked without lowering the glasses.

"Hunters, sir."

"It's illegal to have a gun or to hunt."

"Perhaps other refugees. There are many on the roads."

Müller snorted, then dropped the glasses and pulled out his map again. "We can set up an observation point right here," he said, pointing to a spot on the map. "He won't see us if we keep to the high ground." Having made his decision, he folded the map and walked back toward his vehicle. Fisser and Zarek followed. As they walked, Fisser reached out and pulled on Zarek's sleeve to slow him down and then leaned toward him. "You know that if we don't find him, Müller is going to kill you," he whispered angrily.

Zarek nodded grimly. "He's going to kill me either way."

"Probably. But fail to find the rebel and it's guaranteed."

Zarek stopped and turned toward the sergeant. "Will he kill my daughter and her baby?"

Fisser smirked. "Do you think he'd go all the way back to Gorndask just to kill them?"

Zarek's eyes wandered to the horizon. "The colonel is a hard man to predict."

Fisser reached over and slapped him on the shoulder so hard it almost knocked him down. "Don't worry, Mister Zarek, you're not that important."

Zarek turned and kept on walking. "That's all that I could ask," he said.

Lucas, Cela, and Aron sat around the dying fire. The rabbit had been consumed and Lucas was chewing on a bone, trying to get every bit of meat. Aron sat beside him, his head on Lucas's shoulder. Lucas had wrapped him in the fabric curtain he had torn from the church.

Lucas had removed the pine boughs from over the dying fire, but the smoke was nearly gone now anyway, and it was dark enough that what little drifted up would be impossible to see.

Cela sat quietly by herself, leaning against a tree a few feet behind her brother. She watched him happily, then looked down at her lap, where she was holding a small wooden box. She opened it carefully and pulled out a few of the contents. A braid of hair. An ox-bone comb. A simple silver ring. She gazed at them tenderly, then looked up to see Lucas watching her.

Lucas nodded to the braid of dark hair. "Your mother's?" he asked.

Cela nodded and held up the white comb. "My father's." She reached in and showed Lucas a photograph. It was bent in half, and only the back of it was exposed. "A picture of my family."

Lucas glanced at the mementos, then nodded toward the growing darkness. "It's getting dark. We need to put the fire out before someone sees it."

He stood and started scooping snow onto the fire. It sizzled and steamed, the embers growing almost instantly dark. Aron watched his every move. "It was a good rabbit," he said proudly.

Lucas smiled at him. "Yes, Aron, it was a very good rabbit."

"I caught it."

"Yes, you did."

"I caught our Christmas dinner."

"You did a very good job."

Müller was just getting into his vehicle when his radio man came running forward. "Sir," he said urgently. "One of the patrols has found something you need to know about."

Müller turned. "What is it?" he demanded.

The radio man started to explain.

TWENTY-FIVE

Müller's tracked vehicle pulled into the yard, the SS flags waving from the front bumper. Three German soldiers were waiting between the rock house and the wood barn; they snapped to attention when Müller stepped out of the open vehicle. It was nearly dark, and dim lights shone from the windows of the old rock farmhouse, casting yellow squares across the muddy yard. Behind the barn, the low hills climbed up toward the forest, where the trees were thick and heavy with snow.

A dirty sergeant ran toward Colonel Müller and saluted crisply. Fisser and the German lieutenant stepped out of the second vehicle but hung back.

"What have you got?" Müller demanded of the saluting sergeant without even returning his salute.

"An old farm wife," he answered quickly. "Her husband went out early this morning. He should have come back. But she's seen no sign of him, sir."

Müller waited impatiently. "That's it?" he snarled.

"No, sir. He had some hunting dogs he'd taken with him." The sergeant pointed to the kennels in the back of the barn. "All three of them are back."

Müller scowled, then started walking toward the farmhouse. Sergeant Fisser didn't follow. "Sir," he called out from behind him, "I'm going to go up the hill and take a look around."

Müller waved agreement without looking back. Fisser turned to Lieutenant Acker and motioned toward the high ground. "Will you take a walk with me, sir?"

Acker nodded, and the men started walking toward the highest of the hills.

Fifteen minutes later, they broke out from the dense trees into a clearing at the crest of the hill. The top was completely treeless and the evening sky was clear over their heads. The moon was bright, and stars burned overhead, casting enough light on the snowy landscape to see pretty well. Fisser walked a tight circle as he looked around, then stopped and pointed toward the east. "The Bolsheviks have stopped shelling," he said.

"They're moving their positions west," Acker answered. "They'll be in the streets of Gorndask before morning."

Fisser motioned to the north. "The Russians hit the highway and we folded. We're falling back now like leaves before the wind."

Acker shook his head in near despair. "Which means they're on two sides of us now."

"It might be even worse than that. We don't know what's happened to the south."

Both of them were quiet.

"Colonel Müller knows what he's doing, I'm sure," Acker answered carefully. He kept his eyes on the command sergeant, looking for reassurance.

Fisser didn't answer.

"I've heard things about the Russians," Acker continued. "What they do with captured German soldiers."

Fisser turned to him and smiled grimly. "Don't worry about that. You won't live that long."

Acker tried to laugh, but Fisser didn't smile with him, and he fell silent. After a few moments, he lifted a pair of binoculars to his eyes and moved them across the distant forest, looking for fire, lights, anything that indicated movement there. All he saw was trees. Snow. A winding road and a small village. He could barely see the river in the distance, the water glinting in the moonlight. He finally dropped the binoculars. "We're going to die chasing this last rebel," he said in disgust, then quickly caught himself and glanced anxiously at Fisser.

Fisser pressed his lips together. "Maybe. But there are many inglorious ways to die now."

"Yes, but I want to die for something more meaningful than this!"

Fisser nodded glumly, a moment of honesty slipping through. Acker watched him and realized that he was equally frustrated, and it made him angry. He had expected a rally speech, an "everything is going to be okay" speech. He wanted some assurance that Fisser, or the colonel, or *someone* had a plan. But he didn't get any of that, and he was furious. He had seen enough wasted lives already, and it cut him to the core.

Fisser watched the young lieutenant, pondering what he could say. Half of him wanted to give Acker a bit of assurance. The other half of him didn't care. "It's not up to us to choose our dying," he finally said.

Acker only nodded.

Fisser stared at the horizon and then started to whisper to himself.

How can man die better
Than facing fearful odds,
For the ashes of his fathers,
And the temples of his Gods.

Acker smiled grimly. "I don't see any ashes or temples in this thing."

"No temples here," Fisser agreed as he aimed his binoculars to look west, watching a line of lights along the road. Acker lifted his own glasses and watched the lights. "The triple deuce," he said. They were the last of the German ground forces heading west.

Fisser grunted. "We are alone."

Acker lowered his glasses. "It's hard . . . I mean, the colonel is so . . . determined."

Fisser dropped his glasses as well. "Yes, but we'll get the rebel, I have no doubt. The only question is, will the Russians encircle our position and leave us no way out?"

Acker pulled out a cigarette, lit it, and took a drag. He extended it toward Fisser, who took it and inhaled. They shared the cigarette together as they talked.

"What do you know about your new commander?" Fisser asked.

"Not enough, it seems," Acker answered.

"Not enough, indeed. For example, did you know that Müller was on command staff at the Battle of Stalingrad? Answered directly to Field Marshal Paulus. As cold weather set in, he told Paulus again and again: 'Pull back. Prepare for winter. Wait for a spring assault.' He begged. He threatened. But Paulus didn't listen. And you know the result."

Acker shook his head and reached for the cigarette. "A significant loss," he answered.

Fisser snorted in disgust. "*Utter ruin* would be a more accurate description. Two hundred and sixty-five thousand Axis and German soldiers pushed back. More than a hundred thousand captured. A few thousand of those survived. When Paulus was taken captive, Hitler took his rage out on those who made it out alive. He expected all of Paulus's surviving staff to commit suicide. The fact that Müller had done everything in his power to avoid the loss didn't matter. Müller refused to do it. He challenged the *Führer* to court-martial him and have him shot. Instead, Hitler decided to shame him to death. He ordered Müller out here about a year ago. A fitting end for a failed soldier, chasing a teenage rebel through the forest."

Fisser suddenly paused and lifted his glasses to the horizon. He refocused, then nudged the lieutenant and pointed to the west. "Above the tree line. North side of the road. You can barely see in the light of the moon."

The lieutenant lifted his own binoculars and looked.

"A Russian T-34?" Fisser asked.

Acker shook his head. "No. I think it's a . . . looks like the top of a farming derrick. And it's not moving . . ."

Fisser snorted at himself in disgust. "Curse my failing eyes."

Acker dropped the glasses to his side.

"There's one more thing you might find interesting," Fisser added in a low voice. Acker smoked as he waited, always moving his eyes to scan the horizon.

"Last spring Müller's wife and daughter came out to Warsaw for a visit," Fisser said. "On their way back to Berlin, their train was derailed by the Devil's Rebels. There was a fire. A huge explosion. His daughter was burned to death. His wife survived, but . . . well, she doesn't look the same."

Acker shook his head, then took a drag on the cigarette.

"Interesting," was all he could muster. All of it was so discouraging to hear.

"And I haven't told you the most surprising thing about the colonel," Fisser offered in conclusion.

Again, the lieutenant waited.

"He's never killed a man."

Acker scoffed. "I find that hard to believe."

Fisser took the cigarette, took the last drag, and smashed it in the packed snow beneath his feet. "It's true," he said flatly. "He's ordered many people to die, but he's never pulled the trigger. I think he always considered it beneath him, like cleaning a latrine. But he's saving himself now for the last rebel. That man, he's going to kill himself."

"Unless he kills us first!" Acker voice was angry with frustration.

"Yes. Unless that."

"But that is what's going to happen. He's going to kill us all. That, or we get captured by the Bolsheviks and have our entrails turned inside out. Or we go back and are hung for disobeying orders."

"Unless . . ." Fisser offered, his voice trailing off. He turned and exchanged a knowing look with Acker.

"Yes. Unless that," the officer said.

Three miles away, Lucas stood on another hill. The moon was mid-sky now, casting dim shadows among the trees. It was silent. Clear and calm. The evening breeze had died down. Lucas was alone, the children waiting on the dry ground underneath a clump of trees. He surveyed his surroundings. The terrain dropped suddenly below him to the flatlands. He could make out the road that led into a village and a few farmhouses along the road. Occasional headlights. The sound of military vehicles. He listened carefully, his head cocked to the side.

Behind him, Aron was wrapped in the blanket, shivering and cold. His eyes were closed and he looked exhausted. Cela waited anxiously beside him, her eyes focused intently on Lucas. He turned around and looked at her, his face illuminated by the moon. "We have to go," he said to Cela.

She stood and came up beside him. "You've decided where we're going?"

Lucas motioned to the flatlands, outlining what he was thinking by pointing as he talked. "There's a road at the bottom of this hill, behind these trees, that leads to that village. If the Germans are waiting, they'll be waiting for us down there. I've seen lights along the road, but I can't tell who they are or what they are doing. But it doesn't matter. One way or the other, they're all bad guys. We have to go back the other way. It'll be a little harder traveling, more hills and snow, but we'll be safer if we stay as far away from the road as possible."

Colonel Müller stood in the middle of the small farm kitchen. The interior was dimly lit by a single gas lantern sitting on the wood table. Small and cluttered with old pots and blackened pans, the kitchen smelled of grease and garlic. An iron cooking stove burned in the corner, kicking out a constant wave of heat, and the four German soldiers stood in the four corners of the room. Müller sat in a chair at the end of the table. The farmer's wife stood alone beside the stove. Her face was tense with fear, tear tracks wetting her cheeks, and she clutched her hands at her chest.

All of them heard footsteps on the wooden porch, and they

turned their eyes toward the sound. The woman took a step forward but stopped when Müller lifted a hand. The farmer stumbled through the back door, freezing in place when he saw the German soldiers. He glanced at his wife, his eyes suddenly wide with fear. She looked at him and gasped. His mouth was caked with dried blood, and one eye was black and nearly closed. His wife tried to run to him, but the nearest soldier pushed her back, throwing her against the hot stove.

"We've been waiting for you," Müller said.

The farmer looked at his wife apologetically, communicating with her through unspoken words.

Müller stood up and moved toward him. "Yes, yes, we all know you're sorry. Now, where have you been? And I don't have much time."

The farmer turned to him and stammered. "I was out walking . . . with my dogs. We go out every morning."

Müller reached out and brushed at a patch of dirt on his jacket. "It looks like some forest creature may have gotten the best of you."

The farmer lifted a hand to his face and touched the bleeding bruise on his lip. "Yes, he did," he said in anger. "And I'd be happy to tell you anything you want to know about him."

Lucas and the children came to a break in the trees and stopped. The thunder of artillery boomed behind them, and Lucas glanced over his shoulder at the sound. Moving to the edge of the trees, he suddenly crouched and slid back under the cover of the forest. The children ran and hunkered down beside him. Lucas pointed through the trees toward a farmhouse at the bottom of the hill. It was barely visible in the darkness, a block of shadow and a single light. "Do you see the farmhouse down there?" he asked.

Cela moved a little closer to him. "Could it be the hunter?" she asked anxiously.

Lucas shook his head. "I don't think so. He came up from the other side. But he was chasing his dogs; he could have come up the canyon. If I could just get a little closer . . ."

Cela grabbed his hand. "Don't leave us!" she cried.

Lucas held her hand tight. "But we could hide in the barn. It'll be warm. In the morning we could make it to the river."

Aron leaned forward as he peered through the darkness. "The Germans are down there," he said.

Lucas glanced at him, not believing.

Aron lifted a small hand and pointed. "There's an army truck on the other side of the barn."

"Are you sure?" Lucas asked skeptically.

Aron pointed again. "Can't you see it?"

"No, I can't see anything."

Cela squeezed on Lucas's hand. "You have to trust him. He can see a bird from two miles."

Lucas was uncertain, and he knelt down by Aron. "You can really see them? German soldiers are down there?" Aron nodded confidently. "Aron, looked beyond the farmhouse. Can you see the Oder River?"

Aron moved forward and strained his neck. "I can see it."

Lucas moved anxiously toward him. "Do you see a road? Is there a bridge?"

Aron stared a long moment, then shook his head. "I don't see any bridge."

Lucas stifled a curse. "We are very close now. But we've got to find a way to cross the river," he said, more to himself than to the children. He turned and started hoisting on his pack again. But Aron kept on looking.

"There are some soldiers at the farmhouse," he said in sudden fear. "They're coming up the hill!"

Lucas peered through the darkness, then grabbed the children. "Come on! We've got to go!"

Two squads of German soldiers were moving up the hill toward the trees. They motioned to each other, then split into pairs and fanned out.

Müller stood on the farmer's porch and watched them. His face was intent and scowling. Fisser appeared from the kitchen door, then moved to stand beside him. "Your intentions, sir?" he asked.

Müller turned to face him. "We'll stay here tonight," he answered. "Give the patrols time to see what they find."

Fisser motioned to the other soldiers. "Sir, it might be helpful if we were to position some of our men to the south, along the highway. The Russians are so close their artillery is arching over our position."

Müller lifted an impatient hand. "Do the Bolsheviks know we are here?"

"I doubt it, sir."

"Then how are they going to target us, Command Sergeant?"

"Sir, the point is, the Bolsheviks are moving and we are not. We will find ourselves with very few options if we aren't out of here by morning."

Instead of answering, Müller pulled his small notebook out of his jacket pocket and opened it up. "Command Sergeant," he said, as he turned through the pages, "are we still in range to communicate with our field radio?"

"I believe so, sir, but we haven't turned it on. Your instructions were to leave it off, to stay out of communications until—"

"I know what my instructions were, Command Sergeant. But I want you to reestablish contact with the command post again. The refugee train is coming in the morning. I want to be ready to call in mortar strikes when it arrives."

Fisser clicked his heels but then pressed his original concern. "And sir, what about positioning our men to maintain contact with our own forces?"

Müller started writing in his notebook. Fisser looked down to read what he was writing. *Lucas Capek* appeared in Müller's scratchy writing across the dirty pages.

"We'll stay here tonight," Müller said without looking up.

TWENTY-SIX

Morning broke under a clear sky that was much colder than it had been the day before, leaving frozen crystals to hang like tiny diamonds in the still air. The sun rose above the low hills. A red fox wandered through the trees, stopped, sniffed, then turned and ran. An owl glided between the upper branches of the trees, landed, then spread its wings and flew again when Lucas came into view. He walked over to the children and looked at them a moment. Cela and Aron were wrapped up in their blanket on the bare ground beneath the overhanging branches of a large pine. The soft needles provided a sufficient bed, and the heavy branches protected them from the wind, but they still slept through chattering teeth. He leaned over and shook them gently. "Wake up," he said. "Come with me."

The children opened their eyes but didn't move. Shivering, they held each other for warmth. "It's so cold," Cela muttered. Her voice was exhausted and almost lifeless. Aron closed his eyes again and didn't say anything at all.

"Come on," Lucas said. "We have to go."

Ten minutes later, they stood at the crest of a hill looking down on the winding Oder River, a band of silver that snaked down from the north. Fifty or sixty yards across, the river was dotted with blocks of ice floating in the slow current. The banks were gently sloped, with frozen reeds and marshes on either side. On the far bank, a large grove of trees extended down to the river. Open fields and grassland circled the grove of trees. Beyond the river, Brzeg. Dirty buildings. Brick and wood homes. An old rock church. An abandoned Jewish synagogue. An ancient graveyard on the outskirts of town. On the south edge of the village, a railroad station stood next to a gleaming track. Fingers of water stretched toward the town in marshy bogs and inlets.

Cela stared at the river. "I can't do it," she muttered in fear.

"You can do it," Lucas assured her. "I know you can."

Cela shivered in despair. "It's going to be so cold."

Lucas knelt beside her and pointed to the opposite bank. "It's only sixty yards across. Waist deep. Maybe less. We can make it. I know we can."

"But I can't swim!" Cela cried.

"That's why I'm going to carry you."

Aron stood beside them with his hands on his hips. "You don't have to carry me," he said defiantly. "I can do it by myself."

Cela glared at him, and Lucas had to hide a smile. "Once we get to the other side, we'll move to the trees and build a fire," he said as he pointed to the trees. "The Germans won't follow us across. We'll be safe there. And remember, the train is coming. This is the last hard thing we have to do, but we have to do this, Cela. It's the only choice we have."

"But it's too wide! And so cold!" Her voice cracked with hopelessness. She had been so brave for so long, but she had nothing now to give. She shook her head, then started crying, burying her face in Lucas's arms.

Müller stood at the top of a gentle hill a quarter mile to the east. The riverbank was just below him, no more than two hundred yards away. Half a dozen German soldiers milled anxiously around their military transports. Zarek stood in silence behind the colonel. Müller glanced at him with disdain. He was but a slave, a man clinging to his life on nothing but the whim of his master's voice.

Müller studied the river through his binoculars. Command Sergeant Fisser stood beside him, peering through a set of field glasses of his own. But the sergeant wasn't looking at the river. He faced in the opposite direction, toward the sound of thunder. The approaching Russians. The coming doom of war. "Russian tanks and artillery," he offered in a calm voice. "Three, maybe four miles beyond the ridge."

Müller lowered his glasses and turned to glance toward the approaching Russian army. Without responding, he raised his glasses and turned back to the river again.

Scanning along the nearest bank, he searched for any sign of the rebel. But all he saw were thick clumps of reeds . . . lavender shrubs . . . a small embankment that hid part of the nearest bank . . . frozen chunks of ice jammed along the shore. On the other side of the Oder River, he studied the grove of trees. Beyond that, there was a small farmhouse, but it was too far away to be of any interest to him. Movement caught his eye far to the south, and he turned to see a pair of German military patrol boats retreating along the river toward the German border. He dropped the binoculars and pointed to the receding military craft. "Those will be the last of our patrols." He said it almost smugly, as if he were proud of their position. They were the last ones. The brave ones. Those who didn't *reassemble* to the west.

Fisser watched the patrol boats recede beyond a turn in the river. "I'm surprised to see any of them are still here," he said.

Müller lifted his eyes to the clear skies overhead. "And we don't see any more of the *Luftwaffe*."

"They're hitting the Bolsheviks along the highway," Fisser explained. "I could see them going at it just before dawn. But the aerial battle has moved west. We're far behind the line of our own troops now."

Müller nodded at the forest. "He's out there. He has to be. He couldn't make it to the bridge, not with those children . . ." His voice trailed off.

Zarek stepped toward him. "Unless they're dead," he offered simply.

Müller pulled out a cigarette, one of the few he had left, and lit it without responding. Then he turned and stared at Zarek. "You were wrong about the children," he said. Zarek shifted his feet while Müller glared at him. "Let's hope that you're not wrong about the train. You said it was supposed to leave this morning?"

"Sir, that's what I was told."

Müller grunted and lifted his field glasses again. "They'll have to try to cross the Oder, then," he said. He moved his glasses up and down the ice-filled river. "But could anyone be so stupid?" He stopped, stared, then focused the lens. He pulled the glasses down to check what he was seeing, then smiled broadly and shook his head. "Yes, I guess they could be."

Lucas stood at the side of the river. No shirt. No shoes. His backpack strapped high around his shoulders to keep it dry. Aron was sitting on his shoulders, crying with cold and fear.

Lucas put his foot into the water. Shocks of icy pain shot through his leg. Another step. Another shot. He waded quickly up to his waist and his entire body seemed to cramp, painful knots forming in both legs. He was already shivering from the bitter cold. Chunks of ice brushed against him and he moved against the current as fast as he could. Feeling the shock of the water on his feet, Aron nearly panicked and started pulling at Lucas's hair and scratching at his face. Lucas was in water up to his waist now. Then his chest. And then his neck. The bottom of the river changed from small rocks to slimy mud, and he almost slipped and fell. Feeling him reel, Aron kicked in fear. Only his legs were in the water, but he was shivering from the biting cold. Lucas's face was contorted in pain, and he kept his head down, concentrating on his footing, knowing it would be a disaster if he slipped and sent Aron into the icy water. He leaned forward, keeping his eyes on the opposite side of the river where the high reeds rose up above the waterline. Halfway across. He stumbled. Aron panicked, clawing desperately at his face again. "Aron, I can't see!" Lucas cried through chattering teeth while reaching up to push Aron's hands away. He stumbled once more, and Aron cried again. Lucas doubled his pace until he was almost running. He was shivering uncontrollably now. Ten more yards to go.

He heard the angry buzz just above his head. He knew instantly what it was and instinctively ducked. A spout of water shot up beside him, throwing icy spray in his face. Half a second later, the sound of the gunshot rolled across the river. Another buzz. Another geyser, this one right beside his head. Another echo across the water.

Lucas lunged for the reeds, crossing the last five yards in just two steps. He pushed through the thicket, hit the dry ground, and rolled immediately to his right while pulling Aron from his shoulders and cradling him in his arms to protect him from the fall. Coming to rest beside a small bush, he cuddled Aron tightly and then rolled again.

"Don't move!" he commanded Aron when they came to rest. "Hold still! Don't let him see the reeds move!"

Silence. The sound of lapping water. The rustle of the reeds. Then the ground erupted as more shells impacted fifteen feet to their left. The sound of the rifle shots echoed across the river. Long moments of silence followed. Lucas finally released Aron and lay back, shivering uncontrollably from the cold. Aron started crawling through the reeds and Lucas followed, both of them stumbling into the grove of trees.

Müller's black leather coat was stretched across the snow. He lay atop it, the rifle to his shoulder, his legs extended, his toes dug into the ground. He stared through the scope, moving his field of view up and down the riverbank, searching intently through the reeds.

He swore in frustration. Where had the rebel gone? He lifted his head to look at the riverbank, then bent down and stared through the scope again. He fired another shot and then another, constantly cursing in rage.

Lucas was shivering so violently he could barely move, his hands wrapped around his chest, his teeth cracking in his head. Aron moved beside him, scrambling on his hands and knees. They made it to a small clearing in the trees and Lucas fell, his face tight, his lips already blue. "So . . . cold . . ." he muttered through chattering teeth.

Aron scrambled across the ground beside him, his bare hands sifting through the snow, searching desperately for pieces of wood. "Got to build a fire!" he muttered, his young voice cracking. "Got to get him warm. Got to get him warm."

Lucas shook his pack from his back, ripped it open, and pulled out a small metal canister. His hands were shaking so violently that he couldn't open it, and he dropped it on the ground beside Aron. "Cloth patches . . ." he mumbled through chattering teeth. "Soaked in grease. Use them to . . . start a fire."

Aron grabbed the box, his small hands trembling to force it open. Then he suddenly stopped and looked back through the trees toward the river. "Cela!" he cried. He looked desperately at Lucas. "We can't leave her. Even if they're shooting, we can't leave her!" Tears were rolling down his cheeks.

Lucas dropped a box of matches on the ground beside the metal canister. "Get . . . a fire . . . going," he chattered. "I'll be back." He turned and started limping on frozen feet toward the river.

"Where is he?" Müller muttered as he looked through his rifle scope. He was still lying on the ground, and he moved the barrel of his rifle erratically, jerking from the riverbank to the reeds, from the trees to the icy water.

Fisser was standing over him. "There's nothing we can do, sir," he said. "Unless you're willing to brave the water. He'll be dead in a few minutes anyway. No one could survive that water. That alone will kill him, especially on a cold day like this."

"Don't be a fool! He's coming back for the girl! Do you think he's going to leave her?"

"He's not that stupid, sir."

"That's the problem with war," Müller snorted. "It makes people do stupid things." He lowered the rifle, rubbed his fists in his eyes, then lifted it and stared through the scope again. "He's coming back. I know he will. He's coming back."

"He won't, sir, not now that he knows we're up here. I promise you, he's not going to cross the river again. We can go."

Müller held the rifle still, focusing on one point. He pulled away from the scope and looked above the rifle barrel across the river. "You don't think he's coming back?" he asked.

"No, sir, I don't."

"Then look at that," Müller said, pointing at a black log that was moving across the river. He shook his head in disbelief. "I'll give him this," he muttered as he turned back to the rifle for his final shot. "He's going to die a hero."

He took a breath and held it to steady himself.

Lucas pushed the log against the current. He kept his head pressed against the frozen wood, and the cold water lapped in his face. His arms were draped over the log and his skin started freezing to the bark. A large block of ice brushed against his head and knocked him under, almost forcing him to lose his grip. He heard an angry *buzz* and felt a spout of water. Another *buzz.* Another geyser. The top of the log suddenly exploded from the impact of another shell, sending bits of frozen wood scattering around his head.

He groaned in pain, his teeth chattering so violently it hurt. He peered through icy eyelids to the opposite side of the river. Cela was waiting beneath a bank of dirt where she was protected from the gunfire on the hill. "Lucas! Lucas!" she shouted to encourage him on.

More shots. More spouts of water. He pushed harder, moving the log toward the shore. Cela paced and jumped along the muddy waterline. He pushed harder, feeling the riverbed below him turn from mud to sharp rocks. The water was getting shallower, and he stumbled forward, falling on his knees below the embankment. He crawled forward until he knew it was safe, and Cela dropped beside him.

Lucas was barely conscious. "I'm sorry. I promised I . . . would carry you," he mumbled weakly. "But you'll . . . have to . . . get . . . into the water." His teeth were no longer chattering, and he didn't shiver anymore. His mind was slow. Clouded. Everything was covered in darkness and cold.

Cela looked at him in terror. "It's too deep, Lucas. I can't make it. I can't swim!"

Lucas didn't answer for a moment.

Cela grabbed his hands and blew on them in a ridiculous attempt to warm them. "We have to make it, Lucas! We *have* to make it! I can't leave Aron!"

Lucas pushed himself to his knees and motioned for her to come to him. "Okay, then . . . together. But . . . going to be . . . cold."

Cela didn't wait. She stood and ran into the water. Gasping from the cold, she grabbed the log and started pushing it across the river. Lucas forced himself to his feet, then turned and followed. He fell forward until he was beside her, tossed her onto his back with one hand, then started pushing the log. "Hold . . . to me!" he cried. "Keep . . . your head down. Hang on!"

Keeping the log between them and the gunfire, he started pushing across the river. The water got deeper. Soon he was up to his neck. He was silent as he pushed, concentrating on one more step . . . one more step. . . . He no longer had the strength to hold the log against the current and they started drifting downstream, toward the shooter. He kept his head down, water slapping in his face. He waited for the sound of shells to hit the water.

But the gunfire didn't come.

Müller lay prone, watching the log move across the river through the scope. "He's got to expose himself when he climbs out of the river," he said.

Fisser was also watching the log move across the river. He was completely befuddled. It was the stupidest thing he had ever seen. But he didn't care about the rebel or the log. He didn't care if the man was stupid or a hero. All he wanted was to get away from the Russians before it was too late. The Bolsheviks were no more than a mile away now, so close that he could hear the rumble from their tank engines. The time they had to get away was down to minutes. "Sir," he offered desperately, "I could bring one of our snipers forward. It would be an easy shot for one of them."

Müller pulled away from his rifle and glared up at him. "Do not insult me with your snipers!" he sneered before turning back to the scope.

He kept the crosshairs on the other side of the river, concentrating on the spot where the rebel would have to climb out of the water. He would kill the rebel. He would kill the girl. Then they could go home.

Lucas pushed against the current. They were almost halfway across the river now. Cela clung desperately to him, one arm around his neck, one arm over the log. She suddenly gurgled with a mouthful of icy water, spitting and crying in fear. Her teeth were chattering, and she tightened her grip. "I can't touch the bottom," she cried.

"Hang . . . on . . . me!"

"I can't touch the bottom!" She was panicked now.

"Hang on . . . we are almost . . . there."

Lucas was nearly unconscious from the cold. He could barely hold his face out of the water, and he constantly gasped to catch his breath. Tiny icicles hung in his hair and on his eyelashes. He sputtered and pushed and forced his way forward without looking up. He was slowing down. Slowing down . . . they might not make it . . .

The water started to get shallow. Lucas grabbed Cela and pulled her to his side to keep his body between her and the gunfire. "Stay . . . close . . ." he muttered. He could feel Cela helping to push the log now, having found her footing in the riverbed.

The familiar buzz sounded again, and Lucas jerked. The shot echoed across the river. Lucas fell facedown in the water and Cela screamed. She grabbed Lucas's hair and pulled his face out of the water. The river around him painted bloody red. Cela heard another buzz, and the log exploded around her. The sound of another gunshot echoed across the cold water. Cela lunged forward, trying to drag Lucas out of the river. He lifted his head and started crawling through the reeds, streams of blood smearing down his chest. Hitting the riverbank, he pushed into the tall brush and collapsed.

Rolling to his back, he looked up blankly at the sky. "So . . . cold," he muttered before he closed his eyes.

TWENTY-SEVEN

Müller stared through the scope, waiting for any sign of life, any movement, any scrambling through the reeds. He scanned the brush, the grove of trees, the riverbank, the water. Then he brought his focus back to the reeds again. Everything was motionless. As still as death. A stain of red was still drifting in the water. He focused on it, then laid the gun aside. Standing, he brushed off his uniform, lifted his coat, and shook it. Draping it over his shoulders, he turned to Zarek. "You may go," he said.

Zarek bowed, moved forward as if to shake Müller's hand, then suddenly stopped and turned. He started walking away, and Müller watched him go. "Good luck," the colonel called out in a sarcastic tone.

Zarek kept on walking.

"You're going to need it."

Zarek froze.

"Your people know who you are. They know what you've done," Müller mocked and then laughed.

Zarek kept his eyes staring straight ahead.

"Your blind daughter—her child—neither of them will survive the winter without you. And you, my Polish friend, won't survive a week on the streets of Gorndask."

Zarek slowly turned around to face the German. "I've been told that before, Colonel Müller. But yet, here I stand."

Müller shook his head in disgust. "You stand because I let you. But you won't be left standing once you get back to Gorndask."

"Perhaps, sir. But there is a Polish saying. *Don't curse the day until the sun sets.*"

"Curse it or not, you'll be dead within a week."

Zarek turned away. "The sun has not set," he mumbled as he walked.

Müller watched him go, then turned to Fisser. "Have you made contact with command post?" he demanded.

Fisser swallowed in anticipation. "We have, sir."

Müller smiled. "The villagers here think they're going to leave. Run off to the Americans. I don't consider that an acceptable option for our Polish friends. Do you, Command Sergeant?"

"Sir, there are many things I find unacceptable. But I would say the more important thing now is that we—"

"That's what I thought," Müller said to cut him off. "I find it unacceptable as well. Get the radio operator up here. And get me the coordinates for the rail station in Brzeg."

TWENTY-EIGHT

Cela stood shivering among the reeds, her lips blue, her face tight with cold and fear. Tears fell down her cheeks and she angrily brushed them away, then tugged desperately on Lucas's arm, trying to pull him away from the river and to the safety of the trees. Aron dropped suddenly beside her, out of breath, his teeth chattering. A smear of blood spread down Lucas's chest. Cela looked at it and cried, then reached up again to brush her tears away. Aron held Lucas's shirt in his hands, and Cela grabbed it and pressed it against the wound. "We've got to get him to the fire," she stammered.

"So cold . . ." Lucas started mumbling as he rolled over and tried to stand. Cela reached out to steady him. He struggled to his knees but fell again. Cela bent over him and pulled on his arm again. "You've got to stand," she cried. "You're too heavy! We can't carry you!" Lucas mumbled and rolled over and tried to stand again. Cela and Aron helped him to his feet and they stumbled through the reeds, up the gentle bank, and into the trees. Reaching the clearing, they stopped. Lucas brushed the frozen water from his eyes, looking frantically around. He saw a pile of wood but no fire.

"Fire . . ." he stammered.

Aron was crying now. "I couldn't . . . I couldn't start it. The matches were wet!"

Lucas barely had the strength to point toward his pack. "Flint," he muttered as he stumbled to his knees. Cela dropped beside him, put her little arms around his shoulders, and pulled him close. Aron fumbled for the pack, bent over it, and reached in. He moved his hands around, searching desperately, then pulled out a small block of black magnesium. Rushing to the pile of wood, he grabbed a rock and began to strike the flint. A spray of yellow sparks scattered before him. More sparks. But no flame.

Aron looked over at the others, hopeless tears rolling down his cheeks, then turned to the flint again, striking frantically. Another spray of sparks. But still no flame. His hands jammed the rock against the flint as fast as he could. Another spray of yellow sparks. The patches of greasy cloth finally caught and a whiff of smoke drifted in the still air. He carefully piled on a few twigs and the small flame grew. Aron glanced up to heaven as if to give thanks, then carefully began to place larger twigs and then sticks onto the flame. Cela shuffled toward the growing fire. Within minutes the fire roared.

Lucas opened his eyes and pulled himself toward the flame. Cela grabbed the blanket and wrapped it around his shoulders. When she pulled her hand away she looked down and saw that it was smeared with blood. She looked at Aron, tears still streaming down her cheeks. "You've got to go get help!" she said sternly. Whether from hopelessness, shock, or bravery, her voice was calm now, the panic and desperation having disappeared.

Aron looked at her, his eyes wide in fear.

She pointed through the trees with a shivering hand. "The village . . . that way. Go now! Go get help!"

Aron stood and ran.

Half a mile from the river, the town of Brzeg spread underneath the winter sky. Small and more remotely situated than Gorndask, without the factories to demand attention from the bombers, it was still torn from war. Bombed-out buildings, homes, and highways spread from the river to the empty fields in the north.

The brick railroad station was relatively undamaged, and dozens of villagers were packed together on the wooden platform that lined the west side of the building. Everything about them screamed of destitution. Their hungry faces. Their clothes. Their thin bodies. Behind them, a couple of hundred more villagers were crowded on the streets. A large pine tree sat in the center of the village square, a chain of colored paper and silver stars its only decorations. Though it was Christmas morning, few were thinking of the holy day.

A low rumble began to emerge in the distance. Every eye turned. They could hear it. The hiss of steam. The clang of metal wheels on the tracks. The villagers crowded toward the station. Then they heard the whistle in the distance and saw the pitch of black smoke above the tree line. The train came into view from a gentle turn in the trees, a spot of black metal in the distance.

The villagers started pushing and shoving toward the tracks.

Cela watched Aron disappear through the trees, then turned to Lucas. She leaned over him and wrapped the blanket tighter, but

Lucas pushed it off. He spread the blanket on the snow beside the fire and fell upon it. Shivering, Cela moved toward the fire, steam rising from her wet clothes.

Lucas closed his eyes. "Cela," he said through chattering teeth, "you've got to . . . stop bleeding. I'll . . . be all right, but you have to . . . stop . . . the bleeding."

"What do I do?" she asked him.

Lucas tried to reach behind to touch his back but failed and fell limp. "Did bullet go . . . through?" he groaned.

Cela moved quickly to his side. "How do I know?" she asked as bravely as she could.

"Is there an exit wound?"

Cela rolled him gently to his side, bent over to examine his back, then looked up. "There's another small hole," she said anxiously.

Lucas smiled grimly. "That's good. No bullet left inside me." He lay back again. "How large is the exit wound?"

"I don't know," Cela stammered. "Big as a . . . big as a marble, I guess."

"Okay. I think I only took a fragment. The bullet must have ricocheted off the log before it hit me. Where is the wound? I can't feel . . ."

"I don't know. Just below the shoulder."

"All right, I'm not going to die from that. But you've got to stop the bleeding."

Cela began to fear what he might ask her to do. "Aron went to get help," she offered before he could say it. "We should wait. Someone will come."

"No, Cela," Lucas moaned. "No one is going to come. You have to stop the bleeding." He pointed to his pack. "There's a medical kit. Sulfa. Pour it on. There are bandages." He lay back and closed his eyes again.

Cela didn't move.

"You can do it," Lucas said.

"Help is coming . . ."

"No, Cela. You have to do this."

She swallowed against a tight throat and then nodded. After warming her stiff hands, she reached for the pack, turned it over, and shook it. The contents scattered across the snowy ground. The last of their food. Flares. The medical kit. Her wooden box of memories. The gun. Cela stared at the weapon in surprise, then shoved it back inside the pack. Grabbing the medical kit, she took out the package of sulfa and the bandages and turned to Lucas. "Okay," she said with determination, "what do I do?"

"Tear the sulfa package open," Lucas started. "Use some snow to clean the wound . . ."

She swallowed hard again, then set to work.

Behind her, her wooden box lay upside down on the ground, the contents spread across the snow: a braided lock of dark hair, a white comb, and a folded photograph of her family, the back of the picture facing the clear blue sky.

TWENTY-NINE

Müller stood in front of his military transport, a large map spread across the hood. The terrifying whine of Russian BM-13 *Katyusha* multiple rocket launchers suddenly screamed from somewhere in the north. He lifted his eyes calmly and looked toward the sound. The Russians were shelling the German army as they fled. But Müller knew most of the Germans had already crossed the river on the Byki Bridge. Staring at the cloudless sky, he tried to see the rockets in flight. But it was impossible; they were too small and too far away. Listening to the flying hunks of explosive metal, he thought they sounded . . . he didn't know . . . beautiful. Eerie and unearthly. And though he listened for the powerful *thummppp* of the rockets impacting the ground along the unseen highway on the other side of the forest, he never heard it. The impact zone was too far away.

His men instinctively ducked for cover at the sound of the flying rockets. A few of the rookies yelped like pups and pulled their metal helmets tightly around their heads.

Müller looked at them with disgust, then lifted the radio handpiece to his mouth. "There is a train approaching the station at Brzeg," he said to the fire control officer who would direct the artillery fire. "You have to hit it with our mortars!"

He listened, swore, then shouted into the mouthpiece again. "I don't care about the Russians. That train is the only thing that matters now!"

Cela was wiping her hands in the snow, leaving bloody smears between her feet, when she heard the sound of breaking twigs from the brush behind her. She turned as Aron crashed breathlessly into the clearing. His face was scratched from running through the brush, and he looked desperately around.

Lucas sat by the fire. Bent in pain, he looked up and smiled as Aron emerged from the trees. Lucas had his jacket on, but it was unbuttoned, showing a bloody bandage at his shoulder. Aron ran to him and dropped at his feet. "I found a farmhouse on the way," he said breathlessly. "A boy is coming . . ."

Lucas turned to the sound of footsteps crunching through the snow. A young man appeared at the edge of the clearing. He stopped and looked suspiciously at Lucas, his eyes wide, an ancient rifle in his nervous hands. He lifted the rifle and pointed it at Lucas. "Don't move!" he shouted while thrusting it dramatically.

Lucas ignored him and turned to Aron. Reaching down, he patted him on the head.

"Are you all right?" Aron asked.

Lucas nodded hopefully. "Your sister is a fine doctor."

The stranger took a few steps into the circle. He looked to be about twelve, with unkempt hair, a patched-up coat, and dirty hands. He thrust the gun toward Lucas again. Lucas considered the grungy weapon, then looked into the youth's eyes. "What's your name?" he asked.

"Rahel," he answered carefully.

"I hope you're not going to shoot me, Rahel. I've been shot once already. It hurts."

The young man kept the gun up. They all stared at each other, not knowing what to say. Aron was the first to smile. Lucas looked down at him and smiled too. Cela was last, but she finally broke into a sheepish grin.

The black locomotive spouted steam from the wheel brakes and dark smoke from the single stack as it approached the station. The refugees were forced off the tracks as the conductor leaned out of the side window, waving his hands and shouting at them to get back. The brakes hissed, and the troop cars rattled as the train slowed and finally came to a stop.

A greasy-faced man dropped down the side steps of the locomotive and immediately pulled on the hose to fill the water tanks that powered the steam engine. The desperate refugees watched him for a moment, then rushed forward, pushing and shouting and clawing their way for the doors to the seven transport cars. Children cried. Mothers held their babies close. Fathers cursed as they pushed others out of the way.

The equation was pretty simple. Those who got on the train might live. Those who didn't would likely die.

The panicked villagers pushed forward, but the doors on the sides of the transport cars didn't open. Half a dozen men slipped from the locomotive and climbed onto the roofs of the seven transports. "Get back!" the engineer screamed from the locomotive window. "We will have order. Get back!"

Some of the refugees started climbing up the sides of the transports, hanging onto the metal rods that covered the windows as they scratched their way to the roof of the cars.

A gunshot rang out, and the refugees fell back.

Lucas and the children sat on logs around the fire. Rahel remained at the edge of the clearing, his rifle still in hand. Lucas motioned for him to come toward them. "Thank you for coming," he said in a weary voice.

Rahel gestured to the patch of trees. "You're on my land."

"I think it's about to become the Russians' land."

Rahel finally lowered the gun. "I heard gunshots."

Lucas pushed his open jacket aside and adjusted the bandage around his shoulder. Rahel moved toward the fire, the ancient gun pointing at the ground now. Lucas checked it out as he approached. It had a cracked stock, and the butt was held together with strands of wire. The barrel was a five-sided pentagon, and the bolt action was rusted to a burnt orange. Lucas had no idea how it possibly could shoot. Rahel noticed that the man was looking at his gun, and he moved it to his other hand. "Are you all right?" he asked, gesturing toward Lucas's bloody shoulder.

"It's not too bad," Lucas answered weakly. "I got lucky."

Rahel looked at the desperate children, the bloody bandage, and the smears of red spread across the snow. "You don't look so lucky," he answered.

"It's really not too bad," Lucas said. "It was the cold that nearly killed me. But Aron got this fire going. And Cela doctored me up."

They all heard it at the same time. A terrifying whistle. The sound of German artillery flying over their heads. All of them looked up with terrified eyes. Lucas instinctively reached for the children and pulled them close. Seconds later, an explosion pounded beyond the trees. Another whistle of artillery fire. Another explosion. Lucas struggled to his feet. "He's bombing Brzeg!" he hissed in rage.

Cela looked confused. "The train?" she muttered.

Lucas kept his face to the sky as a third shot flew over.

"The train!" Cela cried. "They're shelling the train!"

Lucas turned to Rahel. "How far to the station?" he demanded.

"I don't know. Ten minutes, if you're fast?"

"You've got five! Take the children! Get them to the train!"

"What are you going to do?" the boy asked.

"I'm going to stop him," Lucas answered. He glanced toward the river, then back to the children. "Get them to the train," he commanded again.

"No," Cela screamed. "You've got to come with us!"

Lucas pushed Rahel angrily on the shoulder. "Go! Get them out of here!"

"No!" Cela cried again.

Lucas knelt in front of her. "Go, Cela," he said firmly. "Go now. This is your only chance!"

Rahel hesitated, looking to the sky, then grabbed Cela and Aron by the hand and started pulling them toward the trees. He suddenly stopped and turned back to Lucas, extending the rifle to him. "You might need this," he said.

Lucas reached out and took the gun. "Go!" he said.

Rahel started running, then turned and came back to Lucas one more time. Digging into his pocket, he pulled out a single bullet. "It's the only one I have," he said bashfully.

Lucas looked at it and shook his head. Rahel smiled sheepishly, then took the children's hands again and started pulling them toward the trees.

THIRTY

Thick fog moved up from the river, stretching its gray fingers along the bogs and the fields but stopping short of the town, leaving Brzeg covered in nothing more than mist.

Through the fog, the children ran.

Ahead of them, the next round of the mortar shells impacted on the outskirts of town. The explosions created instant chaos: black clouds of smoke, exploding metal, clods of frozen earth falling from the sky. The whistle of more shells screamed toward the village, and explosions erupted along the river, in the empty fields to the south, beside the highway, on the southern end of the station. A huge fire broke out in two wooden buildings on the outskirts of town, and the sky filled with black smoke.

The refugees turned to face the incoming mortars. For a moment, they stood in stunned silence. They knew the terror that was coming, the powerful explosions, the fires, the ear-shattering percussions, the blood and shattered bodies. A few of them glanced at the train in disbelief. *The train was here! Freedom was so close!* But as the third shell exploded just a few hundred meters to the south of the station, they broke into a panic. Some of them started running down the street, toward the center of the town. Others stood and cried without moving, knowing there was nowhere safe to hide. Families huddled desperately together, holding each other tight.

As the ground rumbled and the dirt fell, most of the villagers realized that the shells were moving toward the station. The train had to be the target! The few refugees remaining on the station platform turned and ran.

The conductor had climbed out of the locomotive to supervise the refugees. At the sound of the first explosions, he stood in confusion beside his train, a look of terror on his face. Then he started running toward the crew ladder, screaming to the engineer who was waiting inside the locomotive. "Cap the water tanks," he cried as he slapped the side of the engine. "Get the fires going! Let's go! Let's go! Let's get out of here!"

Lucas limped painfully across the snow. One arm hung loosely at his side, jolts of pain shooting through his aching bones with every step. It felt like his chest was on fire, and he was light-headed from the cold and loss of blood. He stopped to steady himself, his head bent, then moved forward, one hand at the side of his face as he hobbled across the slushy snow. He fell to his knees amidst the scattered contents from his pack, his fingers sifting through the slush. Not finding what he was looking for, he straightened up and stared ahead, his mind racing. *It has to be here!* Looking to his side, he saw the pack itself lying in the snow, and he reached down and picked it up. Feeling the heavy weight at the bottom of the pack, he nodded with relief.

He turned and shuffled toward the river, the pack and rifle in his hand.

The children ran through the snowy fields toward the village. Cela clung to Aron's hand and Rahel ran on ahead of them, constantly looking back to encourage them on. "Come! Run! You can do it!" he cried.

The fog was thick across the snowy fields, and black smoke hung like a blanket in the air. Running through the fog, they were surrounded by a constant barrage of ear-splitting explosions, the bursts of fire piercing the gray shroud. Half a mile into their race, Aron began to slow. He was exhausted, starved, in shock, and out of breath. Despite Rahel's encouragement, he slowed to a jog and then a walk. Rahel came back and grabbed his hand, almost lifting him off the ground to pull him along. Cela couldn't see the town through the fog, but Rahel knew where they were going and kept them headed in the right direction. As they approached the town, the fog thinned to a light mist. Another artillery shell whined overhead, and Cela looked up in terror. A violent burst exploded to her right, and she screamed and fell from the concussion. Aron covered his ears and dropped to his knees. Rahel bent over him. "Come on!" he cried, yanking the children to their feet and resuming his mad dash.

The sound of another incoming round raced toward them. Shrill. Piercing. It seemed to scream in anger as it approached at nearly the speed of sound. Cela stopped and looked skyward, her eyes wide, her mouth open in a silent scream. Aron fell and rolled into a ball, tears streaming down his face. "It hurts . . . it hurts . . ." he muttered in confusion.

Müller looked through his field glasses toward Brzeg. The mist had settled over the bogs and open fields, but the sun was rising now and beginning to burn it off. Staring across the river, he had to smile. It was a beautiful sight. The fresh snow. The silver water. The yellow and orange explosions. The shroud of fog.

He pushed the radio microphone to his mouth and started talking. "Take my directions. You're falling short! You need to walk the fire west!"

His soldiers milled around behind him, not paying any attention to the site of the artillery barrage that was hitting Brzeg. They were on the verge of rebellion, their faces tight with rage. They paced beside their transports, staring in fear toward the coming Russian army. It was one thing to die, but to face the entire approaching army . . . and for nothing but one man!

Their rebellion stiffened with every passing moment.

Unable to control his rage, Fisser walked to Müller's side and hissed, "Sir, we've got to go!"

Müller ignored him, concentrating on directing the German mortar team on the other side of the river. "Move fire two hundred meters to the WEST!" he commanded into the radio.

Fisser swore, then turned away and lifted his field glasses so he could look down the road toward the approaching Bolsheviks. A shadow emerged from a small hill, taking shape as it rose above the slope in the terrain. A Russian T-34 tank. And then another. Russian soldiers moved with the tanks, hunkering beside them for protection. Another tank came into view, surrounded by more men.

Acker stared angrily at Fisser, then turned and walked back toward his soldiers, spinning his fingers in a "get ready" motion.

Fisser reached out and grabbed Müller by the shoulder. "SIR! We must go!" he said.

Müller pushed his hand away and spoke into his radio again. "YES! YES! MOVE YOUR FIRE TWO HUNDRED METERS TO THE WEST!"

The children were surrounded by death and flame and fog and hell. The sound of incoming artillery shells. Moaning in the distance. Falling rocks, metal, and debris. Crying children. Smoke and heat and flame.

The explosions were so powerful that Aron's nose began to bleed. Seconds later a group of villagers ran by them, heading for anywhere but the train.

Rahel stood, utterly frozen with fear. His mouth hung open, and he had to gulp to breathe. He raised a hand to brush dirt from his eyes and turned slowly in a circle. He had no idea what to do, where to go, how to protect the children, how to protect himself! But Lucas's words seemed to scream inside his brain. *Get them to the train!* Knowing no better option, he grabbed Cela's hand again, lifted Aron in his arms, and started to run toward the station.

They ran until two shells impacted just before them. Rahel fell, cradling Aron in his arms. Cela fell beside them and screamed, holding her hands to her ears. Mud fell on their heads, a mix of frozen ground and melted snow from the heat of the exploding shells.

A moment of silence followed. Rahel stood and held his hands out and lifted the children. Together, they ran again.

Lucas moved painfully through the reeds along the river. He found a large rock jammed against the bank and knelt beside it, then reached up and pushed the reeds away, providing a clear view to the other side of the river. He could see the open fields along the bank, his own and the children's footsteps creating a trail through the snow. There was a small hill to his right with German military transports sitting at the top. Two men were staring across the river. Others were milling around their transports.

He pushed painfully away from the rock, then stood and moved through the reeds to his right. He heard another round of artillery shells screaming over his head and quickened his pace. A jolt of fresh pain hit him, and he had to stop and bend to breathe. The bones. The torn muscles. He felt as if flames were shooting through his shoulder. He looked down and saw the blood beginning to soak through the bandage. He tugged it a little higher to keep it over the wound, then forced himself to move again.

Staying behind the reeds, he moved parallel to the river, then stopped and pushed the reeds aside again. He was lined up on the hill now, as close as he could get. He slowly crawled forward and found another rock along the bank. Squatting beside it, he lifted the old rifle, loaded the single shell into the chamber, and rested his arm atop the rock, his wounded arm hanging to his side. Looking down the barrel of the rifle, he sighted across the river.

He forced himself to hold his breath as he stared down the rusted sight of the old gun. But he was shaking uncontrollably from the cold and loss of blood, and he had to pull away and catch his breath.

He looked across the river again. He could clearly see Müller standing on the top of the hill. Same black leather coat. Same black officer's cap. Another German stood beside him and, as he watched, the second man reached out and grabbed Müller by the shoulder. The officer pushed his hand away, then turned back to speak into his radio.

Müller pointed toward Brzeg and started pacing, gesturing in rage.

"Almost there!" Müller spoke into his radio. "Another hundred meters to the north . . ."

Fisser watched him angrily. This wasn't about the rebel any longer. This was something else. He knew what he had to do now. He had a responsibility to his men.

Fisser moved to the first vehicle, grabbed Acker by the shoulder, and leaned toward his ear. "Get your men into the transports," he whispered carefully, keeping his eyes on the back of Müller's head.

Müller lifted his glasses again to study the town across the river. Two more shells flew in from the German firing positions along the highway. He watched as they impacted. One of them hit just beyond the train. The second hit a building beside the station, blowing it to bits.

The mist had lifted completely now, and he could see the villagers running in every direction. "One more adjustment," he said into the radio. "One more and you will have the train."

Lucas braced the rifle with one hand and aimed at Müller. His hand continued shaking violently. Taking a deep breath, he held the weapon tightly, his mind flashing back to the conversation with Antoni.

"No one can hit a target at one-sixty meters with a handgun," Antoni had said.

"I can," Lucas had replied.

He sighted down the long barrel to the other side of the river.

"I'll give that forty meters," he whispered to himself. He pulled away from the rifle, twisted off a small piece of dry reed, and threw it up to test the wind. Satisfied, he lifted the gun again. The end of the rifle moved up as he continued to estimate the distance.

Halfway up the hill.

"One hundred meters," he whispered as he exhaled.

To the top of the hill.

"Two hundred meters."

He focused the sight on Müller. "Two hundred forty meters," he whispered to himself.

He drew a bead on Müller, then took a final breath and held it. Exhaling slowly, he let half of the air escape from his lungs. Müller paced again, and he lost his target. He was shaking much too violently. He started over: moved his head away from the rifle, shook his arm, held the weapon loosely, leaned against the rock again. Looking down the barrel of the rifle, he drew the sight on Müller, who had come to a stop while he talked into the radio. He aimed a fraction of an inch above the German's head. A smaller fraction to the left to adjust for the wind that was blowing across the river. He put pressure on the trigger and leaned into the rifle. A touch more pressure . . . a fraction of an inch . . .

The sound of gunfire shattered the morning air.

"I need more rounds on the train," Müller was shouting when the bullet snapped just a few inches above his head.

Fisser jerked around and crouched, his rifle ready. Lieutenant Acker dropped beside him, his weapon also drawn.

Müller remained standing. He slowly turned to face the river, his brow tight in rage. He watched as Lucas stood up from behind the rock, exposing himself above the reeds. The rebel stared at him from across the river, then lifted a hand and pointed at him.

The rebel was alive—and he was mocking! *He was mocking!* The German cursed in rage.

Müller reached down and grabbed Acker's collar, jerking him to his feet and pulling his rifle from his hands. Holding it at his shoulder, he started firing at Lucas while walking down the gentle hill that sloped toward the river.

Behind him, the sound of Russian gunshots erupted through the air. The Russians had finally seen them. Fisser followed the colonel as he walked, his voice raging. "SIR, WE'RE GOING TO DIE HERE!"

Müller ignored him as he walked deliberately toward the river, shooting as he moved. One shot. Two shots. He stopped, held the gun tightly against his shoulder, and fired a third time.

Lucas didn't move. Standing in defiance, he held his arms out, presenting an even larger target for the colonel to shoot.

Müller fired again. The ground exploded three times around Lucas. But still, he stood.

Müller lowered his rifle and ran to the edge of the water, stopping as close as he could get. He raised the rifle and aimed it carefully. Lucas waited on the opposite bank, taunting, his arms still stretched out. Müller knelt to one knee, lifted his weapon to his shoulder, and took his final aim.

Fisser appeared behind him, his rifle in his hands. He lifted it menacingly at Müller's back. "Sir, we are going to go!" he said. His voice was calm now. Determined. Resolute.

"You, Sergeant, will stand your ground!" Müller hissed.

Fisser raised his gun and pointed it at Müller's head. The colonel finally stood and turned to face him. "You're going to shoot me?" he jeered. "You're going to kill your commanding officer? No,

Sergeant, you're going to stand your ground. Just like we talked about. We save no rebel. We save no bullet. We fight until we can't fight any longer, and then we take it like a man. We do everything we talked—"

A single shot rang out.

Müller stood still a moment, a look of surprise spreading across his face. Then he fell forward, a red spot emerging just below his throat. He rolled over and moaned, staring blankly at the sky. Fisser ran forward and knelt beside him. "Tell them . . . move . . . their fire . . ." Müller said in dying breaths.

Acker grabbed Fisser by the arm, pointing back toward the Russians. Fisser stood and looked across the river. Lucas remained in the fire position, his pistol pointed at Fisser now.

Fisser almost smiled realizing the rebel had lured the colonel toward the riverbank until he was close enough that he could shoot him with a pistol. He nodded in appreciation, then lifted a hand in salute.

Lucas nodded in return and slowly lowered his gun.

Turning away from the last rebel, Fisser and Acker ran toward the waiting transports. Reaching the passenger door, Fisser hesitated long enough to look back across the river a final time. The rebel was gone. He climbed into the transport and the tracked vehicle lurched forward, turning sharply to avoid running over Müller's radio that he had left in the snow.

The entire village was frozen in fear, no one daring to move. The villagers looked expectantly to the sky, waiting for the next round of deadly mortars.

But the shells did not come.

The train whistled to clear the track, and villagers started running and jostling back toward the train.

Rahel pulled the children forward. They were close now, closer than almost anyone. Down the tracks they ran. Approaching the train from the front, they ran past the engine, coming to a stop at the first transport car. People were crushing forward, pushing and shoving toward the train. Cela and Aron were first in line. Rahel pushed them up the steps. Cela stopped and turned to face him. "Come with us," she cried.

He shook his head and pushed her up the stairs. Cela stopped and leaned down to kiss him quickly on the cheek. "Thank you," she whispered gently, then rushed into the transport car.

Cela moved to the nearest window and stared through the metal bars, peering back across the fields from which they'd come. Aron stood beside her, craning his neck to see. Cela reached through the bars that guarded the open window. "Lucas!" she cried.

THIRTY-ONE

Lucas limped into the clearing. The dying fire smoldered in the center of a ring of melted snow and muddy footsteps. He looked around weakly, seeing bloody spots and red patches everywhere.

He heard a whistle in the distance. The train was leaving. He had to go.

He saw his gear where Cela had left it, scattered across the snow, and he hobbled forward and started to jam it into his pack. The last thing he reached for was Cela's wooden box.

It lay upside down, its contents spilled upon the snow. A braided lock of hair. A comb. A picture that was folded over. He reached down to pick up the photograph. Before stuffing it into the box, he unfolded the picture and looked at it.

His entire world froze. The air seemed to turn to ash. His lungs filled with cotton, and he struggled to take in a breath. His mouth dropped open and he stumbled back, his balance faltering, his breath coming in short gasps. His vision seemed to blur, and he stared ahead with unblinking eyes.

With trembling hands, he took out his own picture and held them side by side. Yes, they were the same. There he was, a little boy, standing beside his mother and his father. But where his picture had been torn, he could see from Cela's picture that a young girl had stood beside him. Almond eyes. Long dark hair. Melina as a child.

He fell to his knees, his hands clenched at the sides of his head. He closed his eyes and muttered in confusion. And then he heard a voice.

"You did a good thing, little brother."

He lifted his head and opened his eyes.

Melina was sitting on a log in front of him. She wore the same dress and light blue apron, but she was radiant and beautiful, and she smiled at him confidently.

His mind suddenly flashed through a series of jumbled images that showed the passage of his life: Their house. Their family dog. Running through the grass as a child, his father chasing after him, his mother smiling from the doorway, a newborn baby in her arms.

Melina holding Cela on her lap. His father in a uniform. Lucas as a teenager, watching soldiers in the streets. Cela as a little girl, the same curly hair and large brown eyes. She ran to Lucas and coaxed him to pick her up. He held her, and she rested her head upon his shoulder. "I'm going to miss you, Cela," he whispered into her ear.

Another flash of memory: His mother grabbing him by his shoulders and looking into his face. "Lucas, I'm going to miss you! Be careful! Please be careful!"

The memory was replaced by sudden images of war: Gunfire. Running through burning trees. A dying man in his arms.

Explosions all around him. Blurry images of the German field hospital. Hanging on his fellow rebels' arms as they carried him away.

Melina in the church, her face down as if in prayer. She looked up at him and smiled.

The memories faded as quickly as they had come.

Lucas dropped Cela's picture and pushed himself to his feet. He turned to his sister and stared at her, tears rolling down his face. "Melina . . ." he whispered.

"You remember now." She smiled at him gently.

"But you're—"

"No, Lucas. I am not. You know that life goes on beyond this world."

Lucas wiped his eyes, then looked desperately through the trees toward the village. "My little brother . . . my little sister."

She smiled at him again. "You saved them," she said through tears of gratitude. "You saved them, Lucas."

The train whistled through the trees, and Melina glanced toward the village. "You have to go," she said calmly.

Lucas took a step toward her. The train whistled a final time.

"Go!" Melina whispered. "You've got to be with them."

Lucas turned anxiously toward the trees, then looked back at her again.

"Merry Christmas, Lucas," she said, her countenance shining bright as the sun.

And then she was gone.

THIRTY-TWO

The locomotive belched a stream of black smoke as its metal wheels began to spin. Slowly, it started moving down the tracks, steam hissing from the leaking brake lines. The train was packed. But still more panicked refugees were pushing and fighting to get on, many of them crying in despair as the train began to roll. An old man stood in front of the locomotive, demanding that it stop, but the train moved slowly forward and pushed him out of the way. Inside the cars, the refugees huddled together, praying for the locomotive to keep going while giving thanks for having made it on board. Outside, people hung from the handrails, the steps, the metal bars over the windows, anything they could grab hold of to get onto the train.

Lucas came running through the snowy fields just as the train began to gather speed. He held his wounded shoulder with his good hand, trying to minimize the pain. The white bandage had bled through, leaving a large spot of red, but he kept on running, his head down.

Cela peered through the bars and saw him running. "Lucas!" she cried. "You can make it! Lucas . . . !"

The train blew more black smoke and steam. Lucas raced toward the locomotive, but it passed him by. He ran beside the first car, and Cela reached out through the bars. "LUCAS, YOU CAN MAKE IT!"

Lucas reached out for the railing, stumbled, then reached again. A gnarled hand reached out to him, and he grabbed it desperately. An old man pulled him up the metal steps, and Lucas stumbled onto the train.

Minutes later, the children slumped into a corner at the back of the transport car. Lucas slid his back down the wall and hunched on the floor beside them. They sat a long moment without talking, trying to catch their breath. Lucas stared ahead, then turned to look through a slit in the wood on the back wall. He looked back toward the clump of trees . . . toward the open spot along the river . . . back toward Melina.

A long moment passed until he finally turned and stared ahead again.

Aron watched him, then crawled carefully onto his lap. Cela took his hand and held it. Lucas looked down at her and smiled. "Cela, look at me," he said. "Aron. I have to tell you something."

Both of the children looked up into his face. Lucas glanced away, searching for the right words, then turned back again to face them. "Cela, do you remember that you had an older brother? He was going to come home for Christmas, but then he didn't come?"

Cela nodded in confusion.

Lucas pulled them both against his chest. "Your brother has come home for Christmas," he said as the tears ran down his cheeks.

Neither of the children understood. Not yet. But it didn't

matter. They leaned against Lucas and closed their eyes. In moments, they were asleep.

Staring through the splintered slats, Lucas watched the trees go by and then closed his eyes as well.

Outside, the trees were heavy with snow. Then the forest broke, opening up to empty fields. The train moved beside the sparkling river underneath a cloudless winter sky, leaving behind the smoke and pain of war.